Etienne van
in 1954. He
career and he lecturer in the
Afrikaans and Nederlands Department at
Rhodes University, Grahamstown, South Africa.
His award-winning first novel, *Ancestral Voices*,
was published by Allison & Busby in 1994.

MAD DOG

AND OTHER STORIES

Etienne van Heerden

translated by
Catherine Knox

a&b

This edition first published in Great Britain in 1995 by
Allison & Busby
an imprint of Wilson & Day Ltd
179 King's Cross Road
London WC1X 9BZ

This translation and selection first published 1992 in South Africa by David Philip Publishers (Pty) Ltd, 208 Werdmuller Centre, Claremont, 7700.

In 'Bull Factory', David Ogilvy is quoted from his *Confessions of an Advertising Man* (Longmans, London, 1963, p. 61). Joseph Lelyveld is quoted from his *Move Your Shadow* (Jonathan Ball, Johannesburg, 1986, p. 140) in 'Jan Spierewit', which also includes a fragment from the song 'Brothers in Arms' by Dire Straits. Acknowledgement is due to the National English Literary Museum, Grahamstown, for permission to reproduce the photo by Samuel Cronwright of Olive Schreiner's tomb.

A catalogue record for this book is available from the British Library

ISBN 0 74900 112 7

Printed and bound in Great Britain by
Biddles Limited, Guildford, Surrey

Contents

Mad Dog

Jakadas Pool first noticed the rabid dog following their donkey cart on the ninth day of their trek over the Wapadsberg. He was sick to death of staring ahead over the dull grey backs of his two donkeys. The sight of their stupid heads working up and down against the vast nothingness of the plains made him wish that he was back in the valleys of Rooidraai on a Sunday afternoon when he'd come up from the river, washed clean by the shining waters of the Great Fish, and his wife Kintie would rub Vaseline into his hair. Then the first and the very best swig of the thick creamy corn beer from the six bowls standing before the house in the sunshine.

As soon as he saw the madness in the dog, he handed the reins to Kintie, thinking: We're not going to be able to outspan today – not before we've shaken off that scrawny creature. The three children will just have to piss over the side of the cart as we go along. The dog had gained on them gradually, but it kept its distance at about fifty paces. It was a common shaggy-coated thing that could have come from any one of the huts in the Wapadsberg. But the dog was mad. Jakadas saw that the minute he turned round the first time and spotted the dog, with the foam at its mouth, its head skew and the whites of its eyes showing.

'Most likely bitten by a meerkat,' he told Kintie, unfastening his knobkerrie from the cart rail. He tipped the last of the paraffin into the lamp, turned the wick down as low as possible and lit it. He held his oldest child, Fielies, by the ankles while Fielies hung over the back of the cart and fastened the lamp to the rear axle so that it just cleared the ground.

'Right,' said Jakadas, once he'd helped his skinny son pull himself back up on top of their piled-up possessions. 'The smell of paraffin will keep the animal off.' He took the reins back from Kintie and asked her to turn round, sitting with her back to the road ahead, so she could help the children keep an eye on the dog. They were to tell him if it came closer than fifty paces. He wasn't sure what he'd do then. Everyone in the Karoo knew about rabies: even if you were licked by a rabid cow, you got the fits, the fear of water and the foam at your mouth, the lonely wandering and then death, somewhere on the plains, where they had to burn your remains. A meerkat that crept up on you could bite the madness into you. Even if the bark of a rabid dog fell on your ear, said the old people, the germ would get into your head. There was only one thing to do with a mad beast on the farm: run and call the boss so that he could shoot it dead in its tracks.

If they could only find water, thought Jakadas: that would chase the dog away. They'd used the last of their water early that morning, long before the dog had picked up their track. Kintie was near her time and she was always thirsty. The waterbag, swinging from the axle under the cart, was dry; it wouldn't even help for her to hold it against her stomach for the moisture and coolness that might remain in the canvas. Fielies had felt it: bone dry.

He remembered clearly, with the swaying ears of the donkeys ahead of him and Kintie's back against his, how Uncle Danster had fallen foul of a rabid dog in the Camdeboo. Uncle Danster was resting under a kriedoring, minding his goats, when he noticed a draggle-tailed dog slinking up from the lonely plains. The dog was mad, he saw at once: the open mouth, the foaming saliva, the uneven gait. Uncle Danster just left his goats and ran for the nearest water – under a wind-pump about four hundred paces away. But before he was halfway there, the dog got him, just one nip on the shin, before it picked up the smell of water on the breeze and gave way, staggering off into the kriedorings.

Uncle Danster knew he had only three days left on the plains. He drove his goats into the kraal, keeping a safe distance from them, bound up the gatepost securely with a thong and then, from the other side of the wind, shouted his last requests and wishes to his wife and children as they stared at him from the hut window.

For three days all the hut doors were kept shut while Uncle Danster wandered his last wanderings on this earth. The first night they could hear him crying like a jackal, by the second night he was so crazy he came and hammered on their doors. Inside everyone huddled together inhaling the smell of paraffin from the lamps. It wasn't until early morning that they heard him wandering off again – once he had torn all Granny Danster's laying hens to death with his teeth. As he left – Granny Danster always shuddered at this – they could hear his jaws snapping as the fever gripped him.

The third night, when everyone in the huts had run out of food, he came back and ran around the yard on all fours, and the people knew: Uncle Danster had turned into a mad dog and for the rest of his life he would trail anyone who had done him wrong. The morning after the third night, Granny Danster knocked up all the huts. 'You can come out,' she said to the sheltering faces who had opened the top half of their doors. 'The Karoo has taken Uncle Danster, God bless his poor wretched soul.'

He felt Kintie's back stir against his and then she spoke. He knew that movement of her body when she pulled her headscarf low over her brow to speak. 'It's your Uncle Danster,' she said. And in a little while, pulling down her headscarf again, 'What did you do to him, Jakadas?'

He shrugged and tried to joke. 'So I milked his goats in the donga.' But the hollow pit in his stomach also said: Uncle Danster had to choose *this* time – when they'd had trouble over rations at Rooidraai and had to leave the district – to pick on him for the sins of his childhood.

Sjambokking the donkeys to force them into a trot wouldn't help. They didn't have any strength left after nine hot days on the road. And the dog still seemed to be light on its feet, even though its head hung so low. Luckily, Jakadas thought as he looked round, the children were asleep. Fielies lay with his one arm still hanging over the side – he'd been playing with a twig in the spokes of the wheel. The two girls lay in a heap behind the cooking grid and the food tins. Kintie had thrown a sack over their heads for shade.

He still remembered how the old people had followed Uncle Danster's tracks to find his corpse so that they could cover it with thorn-tree branches and set it alight. His tracks went in great circles over the plains, down into the dongas in the dry riverbeds, up against the foothills of the Sneeuberg, but always back to the closed doors of the little mission church under the pepper trees where Uncle Danster had scratched his first name – all he'd ever learned to write – in the dust.

It was the last lucid thing he ever did. The old people tracking him swore that eventually his spoor changed: the footprints round Granny Danster's fowl-run were already half-a-man's half-a-dog's, and those round the thresholds of the huts were a dog's.

And now, on the ninth day of their trek, Uncle Danster had to come back out of the past. Nine days – he could hardly believe it – he and Kintie and the children had already been on the road. At every turn-off with a farm sign they'd outspanned, hobbling the donkeys so that they could graze on the public land on either side of the road. Further than that the donkeys were not allowed – the farmers were pretty quick to shoot a trek donkey. Once the tarpaulin was slung up for shade and there was enough wood to make a fire, he'd set off down the farm road after Kintie had read him the name of the farmer on the board. From some farmers a man simply wouldn't take a job if he could possibly help it. These were the sjambok farmers, who gave you nothing but bokkems, mealie meal and trouble.

He walked alone down the farm roads, and by the last gate, where the trees and flower beds began, the yard dogs had usually started to bark. Then it showed proper respect if you kept your distance, waiting until the boss or missus came out or asked one of the kitchen maids to find out what you wanted.

But there was no work anywhere. Everywhere, trek groups rested at the side of the road. The drought was taking its toll and the farmers laid off workers when there were too many hands and too little work. Then back to the trek at the road. While he was still a long way off, Kintie would stand watching him with one hand shading her eyes, and he'd shake his head so she had time to finish crying before he got back. And when he got to her, down came the headscarf. 'Jakadas Pool, I didn't want to have the baby here on the side of the road; how will the child feel when it grows up and hears it came into this life on the side of the road like a piece of rubbish someone's thrown away?'

On the second day the two hens in the wire cage hanging beside the waterbag had died at the same time, as if they'd been given a sign. That night they'd eaten plump chicken, and again his thoughts had gone back to Rooidraai. If that boss Rooikoos had kept his promise to increase the rations, they'd still be there on the bend in the river with its red dongas full of dassie burrows. But when the boss came down on him in the rations store, hitting him so that he staggered against the maize bags, in front of the other workers, and fell onto the concrete floor and had to stagger up and wipe the mealie meal from his cheek, he'd thrown his tobacco and coffee and bokkems at the feet of the white man, walked home and said to Kintie: 'A man has to be able to hold up his head. Even though you can't raise your fists to a white man.'

His brother Seun had already done two of his three years for assault; it was actually against boss Rooikoos's cousin, Piet Donkerhoek, that he'd raised his fists. They said Piet Donkerhoek caught Seun drunk in the milking shed, singing as he milked with one of the cow's unfastened legs in the half-full milk bucket. They slugged it out right there in the milking shed, slipping in the cowdung and falling into the urine drain, and Piet Donkerhoek's pedigree cows wouldn't let their milk down again for a week. When the udders had swollen hard between the cows' hindlegs and the milk had started to ooze from the teats, they had had to call the vet. It cost Piet Donkerhoek a lot and he lost his quota at the cheese factory because he couldn't deliver milk for two weeks.

Seun's wife and children – she was a housemaid at the big house and the oldest son was Piet Donkerhoek's gate opener – were chased off the farm and the police beat Seun up behind the milking shed before they carted him off in their van. His wife and children lived next to the railway line for three months, stealing food at night from the rubbish bins at the guest house down near the river.

'A person can't stand up to a white boss. You don't bite the hand that feeds you,' Kintie said when he came home the night of the blow. But he'd said, 'A man must be able to hold up his head.' They'd left that night, Kintie crying until they could no longer hear the barking of the Rooidraai dogs. Then she pulled her headscarf down on her brow and the bitter expression settled around her mouth.

They rode until late that night, with the stars bright above them and the white road between the donkeys' heads. He'd used his whip because he wanted to put as much distance as possible between them and Rooidraai before daybreak. Rooikoos might come after him in his bakkie and make him work his month's notice before he left. At the turn-off to Graaff-Reinet he and Kintie argued for a long time. The moon was sinking, and far away over the plains of prickly pear a jackal howled. She wanted to go straight on to Middelburg – she had family in the location there. He wanted to go over the Wapadsberg to Graaff-Reinet because he'd heard they'd had rain there. There would be work.

On the fourth day, when they started up the first slopes of the Wapadsberg, Fielies got stomach trouble from the dead coot they'd found at the roadside. It was only afterwards that they thought: the bird had been lying beside the road all day and no other animal had touched it. They should have realised, but they'd been hungry and pleased with the unexpected piece of meat, and Kintie had made a stew with some bulbs that she and the children had dug up along the side of the road. Fielies was the only one who got sick and for two days his stomach spewed a yellow mess. The coot must have had DDT or jackal-poison in it.

'The child is half dead,' Kintie had wailed. 'That bird was full of poison, the Lord help us.' She hugged her stomach as the crows circled above them and the donkeys moved even more slowly and wearily. Later he'd beaten them raw, only letting up because they simply laid their ears down flat and farted in his face.

'The donkeys are giving in,' Kintie said.

'Mangy trash!'

'Don't hammer them, Jakadas, they are the Lord's creatures.'

He'd also heard that the Lord rode on a donkey, but not like these, not Karoo donkeys, that was for sure.

Kintie looked at him quietly, with her hand on her belly. 'I'm not getting enough healthy food.'

He'd pulled up, outspanned and went to sit under a tree to think – away from Kintie and the children. Going back was out of the question, the boss would have allowed another trek to come in by now. No, they had to push forward to where it had rained, wherever that was.

And, on the ninth day, suddenly: the dog. He'd looked back at the road that tailed off behind them, sat like that for a while and then turned forward until something made him look back again. Suddenly, out of thin air, the dog was there. Whites showing in its eyes, muzzle low to the ground, foam dripping from its jaw. Right between the two wheel tracks, as though they were wires that it had to trot between.

'We can't get down until we get to water,' he told the children. 'If the dog smells water, he'll be off.'

'And if we don't find water, Pa?' Fielies looked up from his game with the wheel spokes. The girls were like their mother, sulky and quiet.

'We will get water. The springs have to come out somewhere. There was lightning in the mountains last night. That way.' He pointed with his whip.

'Don't lie to the children, Jakadas,' Kintie said. 'There was no lightning. I lay awake all night.'

'Under the tarpaulin, yes. I saw the veins of lightning on that side.' He pointed again. 'And this morning I smelt rain.'

'It's dew. You know you can smell dew when the veld is as dry as this. It isn't rain.' And down came the headscarf.

'We'll get water.' He turned back to the front, away from the dog behind them, and poked the donkeys' arses with the butt of the whip. 'Come on, you rubbishes. Gee-up, gee-up!'

The day that Fielies had made yellow puddles on the side of the road every couple of hundred paces, the shearers had come past on their old bicycles. They stopped, leaning their bicycles against a telephone pole. Fielies lay sweating in the shade of the tarpaulin. The six men had a smoke with Jakadas. One of them was a Xhosa and there was also a yellow Bushman who'd learnt to shear in Botswana. The Xhosa went to look for a fat-leafed plant in the veld, and they crushed it and mixed it with a little paraffin and dosed Fielies. He'd slept through until the next day and he was better when he woke.

The world looks poor over Graaff-Reinet way, said the shearers. The fleeces had been soiled by dust storms and any sheep you turned on its back lay splay-legged because of worms. The farmers were paying badly – only sixpence a fleece now. A lot of farmers had bought electric shears. Then one man did the work of a whole team in a day.

To console them, he took out the whetstone he'd inherited from his father. It was kept in some damp rags near the waterbag. 'My Pa was also a shearer, until the sinews in his hand were cut in a fight.' Without saying a word, they took out their shears and honed them while the coffee water hissed on the fire and two herons flew high above them. He'd pointed, 'Look, Kintie, there must be water.' She put her hand on her belly and watched the moisture from the whetstone dry grey on the shearers' fingers.

The shearers had given him a little plug of chewing tobacco before they left, crouched low over their handlebars. They'd heard that a couple of farmers in Somerset East were looking for a gang of shearers. It was still four days' ride away, they had to push on.

'The world forgot about mercy a long time ago,' one said to Kintie. Jakadas and Kintie and the girls had stood and watched the shearers pedalling off into the distance.

'You know how to shear sheep, Jakadas,' Kintie said that night.

'And a house? Are you and the children going to wait on the roadside while I go shearing from farm to farm? The police will pick you up, Kintie.'

'We could look for a house.'

'The farmers only give you a house if you give your labour, you know that, Kintie.'

'I can go and stay with my people in Middelburg.'

'They are already sleeping seven to a room. And you haven't got the right papers to stay in the location.'

The scarf over the eyes. How she'd laughed, on Rooidraai, when he brought her a bowl of prickly pears from the plains.

And now the dog. Even at dusk, still: the dog. Kintie had to hang on to Fielies while he pissed as they rode. The dog trotted over the droplets in the sand, kept on coming as though he'd seen nothing, just the empty waterbag hanging from the axle.

Once, a long way ahead, they saw a cloud of dust approaching them. 'A car!' shouted Kintie. 'A white man!'

They waited until the car came closer. 'We must stop him.' Kintie stood up awkwardly, unsteady on her legs. 'He might have a gun.' When the drone of the engine reached the dog's ears, it lifted its head, pricked up its ears and trotted to the side of the road. But it didn't stop. The sun flashed on the windscreen. Jakadas stood up and waved his arms. Kintie lost her balance and collapsed back onto their things. The car was full of white people. They pointed to the donkey cart. The car shot past. The cloud of dust settled on them. They coughed and the children started to cry. When the dust had cleared they saw the dog, back in the middle of the road between the wheel tracks. 'It's your Uncle Danster,' whispered Kintie. 'He's looking into my eyes.'

The dog's eyes gleamed in the light of the lantern on the axle. Kintie broke off pieces of bread and held out the tin of dripping so that he could smear his bread with it. 'He doesn't come closer even when he can smell food,' said Kintie. The smaller girl had started to cry in the early evening, and although she was now half asleep she still moaned quietly if they went over a bump and the cart rattled. He ate with one hand, holding the reins with the other.

On the slope, the donkey on the left came to a halt, standing four-square in its tracks. He laid into them with the whip, but the donkeys wouldn't stir. Behind them they could see the dog's eyes sink lower as it lay down on the ground. 'He's not coming any closer,' said Kintie. She put the food tins away in the trunk, its lid squeaking in the silence. It was dead quiet in the veld. Everything knew – even the jackals and the crickets – that a mad dog was on the prowl tonight, thought Jakadas. Everything would wait until its tracks had crossed the mountain before venturing out. He got to work with his whip again and suddenly a huge owl whirred low over their heads.

'An owl in the road,' he said without looking at Kintie. She was superstitious about owls. The donkeys moved on again. The owl was probably sitting on the road eating a mouse. Was he imagining it, or could he hear the dog's pads on the gravel? Dew soaked into his clothes, chilling him. Kintie and the children had climbed in under the blankets; she was keeping an eye on the dog as she lay there. He thought about Rooidraai: the moisture on the lower half of the door when he pushed it open to the fresh morning that lay mistily in the curves of the river. The white storks swooping in low over the lucerne fields, at the same hour every morning, before the bees started buzzing among the blossoms and the heat pressed down on your shoulders with its heavy hand.

Rations were scarce, also spare money for clothes or shoes; the hand of the master mean and strict. But a nice farm. On Sundays the police searched the huts for stolen meat or tins of rendered-down fat. The world was hungry, and jobless people roaming the countryside caught and killed the farmers' pedigree stock as though they were slaughter animals. Every Sunday the police van came bouncing over the stones and broken bottles and half-bricks of the track, but the people had hidden it all away: a well-salted haunch of beef in the wreck of an old Ford, on top of the rotten tyre, under the mudguard. Once a whole carcass high in the wind-pump. 'You think the police don't look up,' said the constable – a brown man too, one of their own people – dragging his cousin Willempie away to the van.

As they drove off, cousin Willempie had shouted through the wire mesh of the van just for good measure: 'You'd better set your hare-traps, cousin Jakadas, and tighten your belts on those stomachs!' And the meat in the wreck – the detectives got that because a swarm of blue-bottle flies had started buzzing around the mudguard that afternoon.

Otherwise, beyond the hunger for meat and the gagging on bokkems, they could eke out an existence on Rooidraai. The summer before, the boss had put a tap in near the huts so that they could grow vegetables. After a month or two his patch of tattered mealies was all that was left standing in the dry wind that pushed across the flats from the east. The others' vegetables had shrivelled up or died from the forgetfulness and neglect that come with getting up before daybreak and returning home bone-weary at sunset, to bad-tempered wives and snotty-nosed children. On Saturdays and Sundays Sixpence and his gang fell into a drunken sleep in the vegetables, on the cool spinach and lettuces, until everything was flattened or pissed to death.

And when he said to boss Rooikoos, 'The rations are not enough for a man who works hard with his hands from early morning until late and for a woman and for three children ...', the white man had said:

'But it was good enough until now. What new story is this today ?'

'Our food is finished, boss. And my wife is near her time, boss.'

'And it cost me a lot of money to put the tap in,' said Rooikoos's freckled face right up close to his, 'and all you do is let the youngsters leave the tap open. Look at that bloody enormous pool of water collecting around the tap, and nothing came of your vegetable gardens, even though I gave you seed and spades and everything.'

My vegetable garden is standing, boss, he wanted to say. But in the heat of the moment he let his tongue get away with him. 'The people have lost heart, boss.'

'Why? Why? Because nothing is good enough for you any more? Because of the agitators who sneak off the trains at night and come visiting your huts?'

'Because of the life on the farm, boss.'

'You get houses, you get food, you get work, you get everything. Do you think I get anything for nothing? Where do I get a handout?' Boss Rooikoos in front of him: the red beard, the eyebrows starting to rust – as they always joked over their spades while he walked away from them. The freckles on the face suddenly enlarged, it was so close; he could smell the breath, he could smell meat on the breath, the fat rib chops that Jakadas himself had fetched from the meat room for the kitchen maids to prepare.

'We are hungry, boss. Look how fat your children are.'

And then the flat-handed blow.

Kintie coming with him with her heavy heart. Weeping, she'd loaded the cart and hoisted her heavy body up onto it. Sixpence had given her the tin of dripping – it was left over from the stolen sheep they'd come across in the servitude near the station. 'What's this ewe doing without an owner?' the men had asked. 'Let's fix it up so our wives can laugh again with shining faces.'

When the railway police arrived, the last sinews had been devoured and the last hoof and tuft of wool burnt to cinders. The policemen had looked at the children's bulging stomachs and at the toothless old people sleeping off the feast in the shade of the huts while bluebottle flies foraged round their mouths, and had said, 'Scum of Rooidraai, we'll get you, just you wait. Let us rake out as much as one little sheep's horn from the ashes in your hearths, and every one of you will land up in front of the magistrate.' But everything was burnt away and human droppings are just human droppings – the detectives realised that when they went to investigate in the donga behind the aloes. The ewe disappeared into the hungry bellies of Rooidraai and came out the other end as nothing.

He smiled, and then noticed that Kintie was lying with the children. He looked back: there were the eyes, the eyes that would not leave them. Eyes he remembered from the dreams of his boyhood when Uncle Danster turned into a dog: you're sitting in the veld, completely comfortable, when suddenly a tame meerkat shows up and you think he'll run away when he sees a person, but as he gets closer, your second thought is that this must be a pet that's wandered away from its home, and before you have a chance to look it in the eye, it attacks you with foaming, gaping jaws, scrabbling claws, biting the madness into your flesh. And now: he pretended he couldn't hear Kintie crying from where she'd burrowed her head in-between the children. Over the sound of the donkeys' hoofs he could now clearly hear the crunch-crunch of the dog's paws.

'The owl,' Kintie said, sitting upright when he turned round again.

At daybreak, as the dog grew clearer in the dim light, they arrived at the top of the Wapadsberg. The winding pass slipped down, and stretching far over the empty plains they could see a mistiness collected. 'Dry mist,' he said to Kintie. They started to go down, he pulled both sets of reins in tight, the donkeys braked back in their bits, swaying their heads from side to side as though they were trying to see past the blinkers. The shaft lay high against their necks.

'There's a farmyard!' he shouted suddenly. The sun flashed on the roof of a house between tall trees. 'Kintie, get out the bread and the fat, we're going to that farm.'

Kintie was beside him, her eyes shining with excitement. 'The food is finished,' she said, but it didn't matter any more. Fielies started to cry when he heard, and Kintie got nauseous and vomited over the side of the cart. He heard the retching of her empty stomach. He didn't look round: the dog would step over the stuff from her stomach without even sniffing at it, he knew.

Down on the flats they turned into the farm road.

'Paradise Valley,' read Kintie.

'And the boss? And the boss?'

'The name isn't clear,' she answered. 'The paint's worn off.'

Slowly they rumbled up the farm road with its avenue of trees. The dog also took the turning at the signboard and followed them.

'Is that mongrel still coming?'

Her silence answered his question.

The farmyard gate was open so he needn't have sat and planned how he'd have to leap off to open it. The gardens were a bit neglected. Jakadas looked round at the dog again. Kintie and the children were clustered round him now. He could feel her stomach pressing against his back. Bright sunflowers stood next to the road, some of them bent by the wind.

The doors of the wagon shed were open. It was empty. Kintie drew in her breath. 'There's no one here, Jakadas!' she grabbed hold of him, her fingers in his ribs. 'Oh, Lord, Jakadas, the owl told us that, the dog is going to get us right here.'

He had to think quickly. There wasn't a road round the house. There was space to turn the donkeys, but only the one road out. He looked round. Fifty paces back, between the tracks, head hanging low: the dog.

'We're going into the house,' he said.

Kintie gasped. 'That's breaking in. The police ...'

'Shut up, Kintie.' He slapped the children to make them stop their crying and aimed a slap at Kintie too. Then he looked back again. The dog was a good way back, foam splashing from its red tongue onto the teeth.

With two vicious cracks of the whip, he spurred the donkeys quickly up to the front door, throwing the reins to Kintie and leaping off. He looked back but couldn't see the dog; it must have been somewhere behind the cart and the donkeys. With his first kick the door creaked. It was made of tough wood. With the second Kintie started to cry. With the third the wood cracked round the lock. He shouldered it open. Kintie passed the children down, first Fielies, who was tossed head over heels into the house, then the two girls, then Kintie, heavy and clumsy in his arms and her breath sour from the vomiting on the mountain pass after they'd seen the farmhouse.

Just before he slammed the door shut and pushed a chest against it, his eyes searched for the dog but there was still no sign of it. Nervously they looked round the dim house. The furniture was grand: copper ashtrays and vases, a big portrait over the fireplace, deep easy-chairs. He wiped his mouth with the back of his hand. A white man's house – he could smell it: floor polish and meat in the kitchen. Soap, fly spray. Thick carpets on the floor and, in front of the fireplace, a leopard skin with a stuffed head. Open mouth and glass eyes. He shuddered and looked out. The donkeys stood in their harness, grazing on the lawn, unaware of the dog and the cart that joggled comically with their movements. The dog lay in the middle of the yard with his head on his paws and his eyes fixed on the front door.

Kintie and the children went down the passage ahead of him. In the bedrooms beds were neatly made up. In the bathroom, with its snow-white black-lidded lavatory, the children sucked thirstily at the closed tap. When Kintie opened it, clear water splashed over their faces. Fielies stuck his head under the tap and laughed at the water that rinsed over his dusty neck and ran in a brown stream into the white bath.

Jakadas pushed the pantry door open. Thick, heavy biltong – back strips – hung from the ceiling. There was a half-opened sack of yellow-gold dried peaches. He took a handful and popped them into the children's cheeks. Kintie turned and stood before him with a tear-stained face. She looked down at the children and then back at him. 'Today we are stealing, Jakadas, in the eyes of the Lord.'

He found some kindling and a few pieces of firewood in the corner, stuck them into the stove and fetched a box of matches from the pantry. When the flames were roaring in the black stove, Kintie put a mug of coffee before him. He cut long strips of biltong. They stayed in the kitchen with all the food until they'd eaten their fill. It was late morning when Fielies fell asleep on a sofa in the living-room. Kintie let the two girls bath in the white bath. They soaked in water up to their shoulders, their small bodies brown against the white enamel. Jakadas's fingers caressed the smooth, glossy tiles.

Later, when the children were all asleep, he and Kintie went to the sitting-room at the front of the house.

'Where's your Uncle Danster?' she asked.

Jakadas looked outside.

'He's lying in the yard, watching the front door.'

Kintie looked at the portraits on the wall. 'Your uncle,' she said, 'did he have a reason to harm you?'

He shook his head. 'No.'

Kintie took his arm. 'Let's get some rest, Jakadas.'

They slept the whole afternoon and right through the night. When he woke up next morning and peered through the window of the front room, the dog was gone. He checked from the other windows but there was nothing to be seen. Then he filled a bucket of water and, while Kintie waited anxiously at the front door, he stepped out into the yard. He gripped the bucket tightly, ready to throw it.

He looked first at the place where the dog had lain. The gorged donkeys dozed in the shade of a bluegum in the garden. Donkeys' hoofprints and the marks of cartwheels were clear in the gravel, leading up to the front door and away again, through the yard gate. Their footprints – his and Kintie's and the children's – lay crookedly round the front door where they'd jumped off the cart and gone inside so quickly.

Jakadas went back to the house. Kintie opened up for him. 'The mad dog has gone,' he said. 'Probably to go and die in the open.'

It wasn't until late that evening, when the children were asleep with full stomachs and he and she were sitting in the bath together and he was rubbing her round, swollen belly with white soapy lather – it wasn't until then that he told her that there were no dog tracks.

The Bull and the Bishop

It was unnaturally quiet, deep in the Karoo at ten o'clock in the morning in this small town named after an English governor from the colonial era. Buses from far and wide were homing in on the township. They appeared over the hill above town, like giant caterpillars, crawling ponderously along the quiet streets and through the deserted business centre. Only one solitary Greek stood in a white apron on the veranda of his shop, as if to say: I am not involved, that is why I am here.

The buses followed the yellow lampposts that indicated the main street. Some went astray. One even drove by accident into the yard of the girls' school hostel. The pale faces of girls from farms in the vicinity peered out through closed windows.

The buses emerged from the town on the eastern side. Railway houses made up the town's last white neighbourhood and from here the residents could see Casspirs gathering where the tar road slipped, smooth as soap, over the side of the hill. The soldiers detailed for surveillance of the township could see the soccer fields where the mass funeral service was to be held. They also had a view of what had come to be known as Stone-thrower's Lane – the gravel track that circled the south end of the township and led to the farms along the river. In the poor railway neighbourhood adjacent to the township, the people had locked their doors and fastened their windows securely. Even the dogs had been brought inside: you never knew when the black hordes might begin to march, and what if it were your dog that barked at them over the garden fence? Next thing it would be your fault that – as the town clerk had put it in a circular – 'the spark landed in the powder keg'. Nonetheless, the crackle of walkie-talkies manned by the soldiers in the Casspirs was reassuring to the people in the railway houses.

After leaving town on the eastern side, the buses revved up the slight incline, past the Casspirs parked on the side of the hill. Some of the passengers looked at the soldiers, others looked away. Many sat nodding in their sleep, for they had travelled a long way. A single Black Power clenched fist appeared in the second-to-last window of the third bus. The soldiers sat immobile, their firearms and teargas launchers gripped between their knees.

On the slopes of another hill at the northern end of town, the rich people in the smart area could just about see over the rise with the railway housing if they looked from their upstairs windows. They could watch the buses pulling up, but the soccer fields were out of sight and the black masses swarming from the buses disappeared behind the humps of rocks on the hill. The rich people stood on their balconies; a couple of them even climbed onto the roofs but had to be satisfied with staring at the empty buses and eventually pointing out the cloud of dust that rose slowly into the air above the hill as tens of thousands of people converged on the funeral ground.

Farmer Tokkie Nel experienced a premonition of loss as he stood at the station watching the vet check that the newly-purchased stud bull could be declared fit and fertile. They stood in the railway pen because Tokkie refused to take possession of the animal until the vet, who had looked after his herd for two decades, confirmed that the long journey had not taken its toll.

The vet looked into the animal's choleric eyes, stroked

the dimpled flanks, felt the penis and let the two huge testicles rest in the palms of his hands for a minute before raising them a couple of centimetres. Then he looked up at Tokkie, who was standing by anxiously on the platform. With the testicles in his hands he grinned and said, 'These must be the two most valuable economic units that you've ever owned, Tokkie, except, of course, your own …'

Tokkie only nodded at the joke. This morning he had a sense of impending doom. Even his workers, standing about, kept looking over their shoulders in the direction of the location. He'd had to take out an extra mortgage bond on the farm to make up the forty thousand cash he'd handed over for this Jersey. It made one shudder to think of what it would cost to import breeding stock of this calibre at the current rate of exchange.

And he hadn't found the time to have this new possession endorsed on his Multiplex. Actually a bit irresponsible: it was a long drive to the farm, along Stonethrower's Lane as well, and then on a gravel road because the Casspirs had blockaded the tar road past the location. Over all the single-lane bridges which gave you the horrors if you were stone-cold sober at the wheel of a five-tonner and all the young farmers were dashing about drunkenly in their Datsuns or Ford Bantams. Then along the stretch of sandy track where the river had overflowed last year and then, thought Tokkie, not without some anxiety, the five-tonner had to negotiate the bends in the pass, where the view could lure a man to sudden and certain death.

The bishop in the passenger seat of the leading car wiped the sweat from his brow with a white handkerchief. He waited until the coffins were carried out from behind the pavilion – five lily-white coffins with photos of the deceased positioned on each one together with flowers and the ANC colours – and then he climbed out. The ululations that broke out at the appearance of the coffins swept him bobbing through the crowds. Behind him, a couple of other church leaders got out of their vehicle. The last two cars belonged to foreign embassies, and the diplomats inside them screwed up their eyes against the harsh African sun and the dust stirred up by thousands of feet. They weren't particularly high-ranking – third secretaries at the most – but their presence lent international sanction to the event.

The bishop climbed up onto the platform and raised a clenched fist. He was an imposing figure in his ankle-length scarlet robes with a huge silver cross hanging round his neck. He was a black man, born and bred in this area.

As a little boy, he was very fond of recounting, he had made wire cars and sold them to the children of white tourists who stopped at the little tables under the shady trees next to the highway to Port Elizabeth. This was how he had earned the money to buy his first bicycle, which in turn enabled him to run errands for the Chinese general dealer in the township. Later he had bred rabbits, once again selling them to the white children in town.

His ultimate ambition had been to open his own shop, but he was frustrated by the maze of regulations that controlled black business initiative. Then he accepted a bursary from a local church, went to university and finally travelled overseas on a study grant. He had risen to the elevated position of bishop: a well-spoken man who had combined his political instinct with an innate sense of showmanship. His fierce commitment to liberation theology had made him the ideal choice to officiate at countless political funerals – and this in tandem with his demanding ecumenical programme.

When he personally hooked the bullhook into the ring in the bull's nose and led the animal carefully onto the platform, Tokkie felt a glow of satisfaction in spite of his premonitions. This was a hot number, he thought, a worthwhile successor to Ferdinand, who had valiantly jumped over the kraal fence on a Sunday afternoon when they had all overeaten and lay negligently sleeping. As the bull was helped solicitously up the gangway into the rear of the truck, farmer Tokkie shuddered anew as he remembered how the patriarch of his stud had bellowed that afternoon. Ferdie was in the yard goring a haystack in his rage and pain. And there, on the barbs of the top strand of the wire fence, like enormous loquats, hung Ferdie's economic units, as the waggish vet called them. With one mighty leap, Ferdinand had crossed the grim divide between bull and ox.

Keeping Ferdie for the aesthetic pleasure he might afford the eye was out of the question. With the hormone imbalance, his handsome form would soon sag into the full roundness of an ox. But the worst would be the eyes without rage or lust.

The matter was settled with a single, heart-rending shot from farmer Tokkie's 30-06, scrupulously cleaned and oiled to ensure an instant and painless death.

And now, bad-tempered and capricious, the new heavyweight. A worthy but terribly expensive replacement.

An unnerving possession, thought Tokkie at the five-tonner's steering wheel as he drew off cautiously, watching the waving vet, the goods clerk and the stationmaster in his rearview mirror. Four black hands had shoved the bull onto the truck, his hindquarters were secured with rawhide thongs, and chunks of foam rubber thrust between thong and priceless flesh. He was blindfolded as a precaution against car-sickness and his head was securely haltered to the rails behind the cab.

Exhausted after a night of negotiating with the security police – they'd arrived unexpectedly at his house to arrest his own son – the bishop looked out over the crowd and prayed there'd be no incidents like there'd been at the last funeral gathering when one of the mourners was necklaced with a petrol-filled tyre and had been forced to set himself alight. A crumpled, distorted scrap of charred flesh was all that had remained as the ululating crowds danced for the television cameras. He shuddered and prayed silently while he waited for the roar of jubilation to subside. He could not see the furthest members of the horde: forty paces away the faces disappeared in a haze of brown dust. But, without counting, he could feel the breath of thousands of lungs around him, thousands of ears pricked up to catch the first words from his lips, thousands of hearts beating for liberation in varying degrees of rage and frustration. Whether he was wearing the correct uniform for this liberation, the bishop didn't know as he waited for the crowd to settle down. He thought of his son thrashing about between the two security men.

Farmer Tokkie Nel stopped at the service station on the southern outskirts of town. He had to wait a while until the service-station manager appeared at the window of his small office, peered out, unlocked the door from the inside, and came towards him over the forecourt. They shook hands.

'Everything that is black is at the funeral today,' the man said to farmer Tokkie. The farmer unscrewed the petrol cap while the other man unhooked the hose. Together they filled the tank with petrol. At the sight of these two white men working so close to them, the two workers on the back of the truck removed their hats respectfully. The bull lifted his tail and great pods of steaming green dung issued from his nether regions to plop onto the floor of the truck. The workers sprang aside, shaking their heads.

'Listen,' said the manager to Tokkie. They pricked up

their ears: the chanting from the township descended like a swarm of locusts on the roofs of the quiet town.

Three of the Casspirs had edged nearer to the soccer grounds – so that they could form the advance guard if the crowd decided to march into the white business centre in protest against the one thousand people detained under government emergency regulations. Earlier, when the line of official cars with the church leaders and diplomats had arrived, the crowd began to sing and mill about like ants from a damaged anthill. But it was actually the waving arms and nodding heads that made it seem as though the horde was moving constantly round and round, the officers on the Casspirs realised.

Through his binoculars the commanding officer could see how banners were hurriedly unfurled when three, four – no, five black cars appeared from behind the soccer stadium. He studied the banners: the banned colours of the ANC, the slogans of trade unions and workers' organisations and, right up front near the platform, the red banner of the SACP. Trade union leaders and the organisers of resistance movements were now putting in an appearance, the soldiers realised, uneasily fingering the barrels of their guns. The crowd began to chant as the cars nosed their way through. A few youths beside the coffins produced imitation AK-47s, fashioned from wooden posts ripped from a municipal fence.

When the cars drew up at the coffins, the chanting and ululating rose to a deafening crescendo. The morning was practically windless, but now the dust cloud started to drift slowly over the white residential area so that a couple of hayfever sufferers had to hold handkerchiefs over their noses. A good fifty to sixty thousand people, reckoned the commanding officer, while he focused on the foreign press contingent clustering round the cars, with video cameras on their shoulders, stills cameras festooned round their necks and long tubular microphones under their arms.

He was thankful that the two black workers on the back of the truck were tame – a pair who'd been in his service for years and had several times made a point of saying they had no time for the agitation in the location. On leaving the service station, farmer Tokkie swung down into the empty main street and turned into the gravel road that led via Stone-thrower's Lane to his farm. He sucked on his pipe, keeping the vehicle in third gear, dreaming of the extra calf pens he would fence off, in a neat line in the shade of the pines next to the new bull's stall, so that he could see his offspring every day.

He'd been lucky to get the assistance of the station foreman and goods clerk because the railway workers hadn't shown up: they were probably sitting like frightened fowls in the railway houses with whatever firearm they could lay hands on, lying on the table in front of them. One old chap had pitched up at the hardware store with a Mauser that looked as though it hadn't been used since the Anglo–Boer War. He wanted someone to drill the rust out of the barrel.

It was hard to believe, thought farmer Tokkie, just as he entered Stone-thrower's Lane, that it was here on this very eastern border, beside this very river, that our forefathers, generations back, had dug in their heels against the Xhosa. With a wagon or two, a couple of muzzle-loaders and a bunch of mongrel dogs. How soft the *volk* had become, written soft by the liberal press, thought soft by a guilty conscience, decided Tokkie, in second gear now.

I am one of the few, thought Tokkie, watching the flaring nostrils of his pricey stud bull reflected in the rearview mirror, who have a high regard for the *volk*.

The bishop thought about what he'd told his son earlier:

Christ did not promise us victory; Christ promised us life, and with life goes death. His son, home from a university campus that had closed because of a boycott, sat and looked at him without saying a word. How could he explain? He – who at that age was selling rabbits to white children – to his son who had all the options of protest? That to hope for victory, to strive for victory, to shed your blood for liberation, didn't mean that you had also to judge yourself in terms of success or failure?

He looked at the crowd who were waiting for his words. He felt anxious because when he arrived, he'd seen the Casspirs against the rise, the soldiers sitting motionless under their helmets, the officers standing in front of the vehicles.

Did he have to explain that there came a moment when one no longer hankered after reward? That all you hoped for was the daily experience of peace and the power of faith? How did he explain this to his son who, as a ten-year-old in 1976, had watched the seniors of his school yield to the bullets? And if his son looked him in the eye and said: Neutrality is not possible in any crisis? How neutral was the love of God? Was it a love without a dynamic? A passive love, complete in itself, at a remove from the people who stood before him now, waving their fists in the air and looking for a sign from him, before returning to their hovels of iron and patched canvas? Was the earth owned, as his son said, by General Motors and Anglo American and the United Fruit Company? Where was the just hand of God who was going to give education, food, clothing and liberation to the millions in the townships?

The bishop thrust out his fist as an answer to the crowd. I, he thought, am a prisoner of love.

Just outside town, before he entered Stone-thrower's Lane, Tokkie Nel had realised that the bull – Lomoteng Winston of Jersey – was growing restless. He was tossing his head, banging his horns against the railings. The farmer pulled up, and when he switched the engine off he could hear the uproar in the township. Once he'd got out and seen for himself that the thongs were still secure, he drove on.

But as if fate was determined that the anxiety that had plagued him all day must have some justification, the bull sank to his knees as they rounded a bend on Stone-thrower's Lane. For one ghastly moment it seemed that the bull would break his neck, because his head was tied fast to the railings. Tokkie slammed on the brakes, yelling to the workers, 'Get him up! Get him up!' The workers tried to get through between the bull and the rails, but with the sudden braking, one of the thongs snapped like a gunshot, the bull jerked his head free, stood still for a second and then instinctively started to back away. The rear rail gave way as farmer Tokkie leapt from the cab. 'Stop him!' he bellowed, but the bull had already broken through the railing and fallen from the truck with a mighty bellow, hindquarters first. Farmer Tokkie sprang to one side and the workers hung on to the side rails for dear life.

Blindly, the bull made off into the veld, crashing into a thornbush, staggering over a tussock, rubbing his head against the ground to get the blindfold off. Finally the cloth came loose and the bull charged off, into the shallows of the Fish River, through the sparkling water, his hoofs sending up showers of spray into the sunlight. Then he was out on the other side. As if he was searching for a target for his rage, Lomoteng Winston of Jersey stormed onto the soccer grounds where the thousands of mourners had gathered together. From beside his five-tonner, farmer Tokkie watched, desperate and helpless.

'He slipped in his own dung, boss, and then the thong broke,' said one of the workers.

'Come on,' answered farmer Tokkie, 'Come on, we must

get him.'

Through his binoculars the commanding officer saw the bull coming. Even he, a townsman, could see by the proud carriage of the head that the animal was well bred. As the furious bull approached the township the sun shone on his flanks. 'Look at that,' said the commanding officer to his colleagues, and in an instant all binoculars were focused on the bull. The animal was making rapid progress, and when the commanding officer swung his binoculars to the soccer grounds and then, after a minute, back to the bull it had moved round towards the big group of Casspirs, targeting on the small vanguard contingent positioned a couple of hundred yards closer to the gathering.

With all possible speed, Tokkie Nel raced through the quiet town. The Greek appeared on his veranda, cleaning his hands on his apron. 'Bloody workers,' swore farmer Tokkie. 'Can't even keep an eye on a haltered bull.' He jumped all the stop streets, and in the railway area the people thought it must be an army vehicle roaring along like that. To their surprise it proved to be an ordinary farm vehicle with two workers on the back and a farmer with hat and pipe at the wheel. It got more dramatic when the truck drove straight through the road blockade, throwing a young soldier onto his backside and sending a drum and a plank flying. All binoculars now swung to farmer Tokkie. The commanding officer was struck dumb for a moment when he saw that the heavily sunburnt forearms and hands gripping the steering wheel were unmistakably white.

The bull had now come to a standstill in front of the V-formation of advance Casspirs. Tokkie quickly caught up and, when the bull realised the truck was behind him, he made as if to charge the group of officers beside the

Casspirs. Somewhat astonished, the officers jumped up into the vehicles. They were even more surprised when they saw farmer Tokkie's truck approach, swaying between the obstacles of burnt-out cars, wrecks and shards of half-melted glass where petrol bombs had earlier exploded on the hard-trodden township road. On the back of the truck, each with one hand on his hat and the other anxiously gripping the railings, stood the two workers. The bull withdrew once the officers were aboard the Casspirs, but now charged again. He pawed the ground and gored it with his horns, found an opening and charged through the formation.

'Bloody Casspirs,' snarled Tokkie between clenched teeth. He was bracing himself to get through the blockade with a deft swerve, because he could already see, between the Casspirs, the brown shoulders of his expensive and enraged Lomoteng Winston of Jersey as he charged on the tens of thousands of blacks who were inciting the bishop with raised fists.

All at once the bishop realised that the crowd had smelt blood. Experience had taught him to discern it in the very breath breathed around him. In the ululating voices of the women and the roar of the men and the trembling of the earth under his feet he could feel that a united energy was focused on something. He wiped the sweat from his brow, and took hold of the silver cross on his chest, suddenly lying cold in his fingers.

Once again the memory of the night before came to him, how the police had bundled his son into the vehicle, how he'd thought: Christ overturned the tables in the temple, of all places. Christ: rage. He had lain awake all night trying to reconcile the two ideas. His almost Catholic predilection for tangible symbols of his faith had kept him staring at the crucifix above his bed for a long time: the heavy eyelids, carefully carved from wood by a cripple at a mission station in the north; the sinewy arms that spread wide with a dancer's grace, given over to martyrdom; the pierced hands, the frail rib-cage. Christ, he thought. What a radical love you exact from me, Lamb of God, splayed-open son.

As one body the officers brought their loudhailers to their mouths to call him to his senses, just as Tokkie Nel wrenched his five-tonner into second gear, threw a tight curve round the V-formation and drove into the crowd, praying that his bull would be spared slaughter. Even in his alarm and anxiety he was aware that above them a pall of dust had risen against the sun. Behind him one of the officers considered instructing a sharpshooter to take out the rear tyres of the truck, but the chance that a stray bullet might hit one of the crowd decided him against it. Even the crack of a single shot could stir the masses up, and their orders were to keep a low profile. Another officer considered following the farmer in his Casspir, but realised what an effect it might have on the crowd if a Casspir suddenly advanced on them.

The rear section of the crowd had noticed the bull and the farmer bearing down on them. Fired by the new diversion, they turned. At first it was a joke, but then the last row realised the bull meant business. A wave of faces turned away from the funeral platform. They couldn't see anything, but they could hear shouts and the engine of a large vehicle. Farmer Tokkie took off his hat, laid his pipe down on the seat beside him and slowed down. The bull too stopped in its tracks. 'Keep your head, Tokkie Nel,' said farmer Tokkie to himself.

The bishop realised something was afoot beyond the cloud of dust. Even in the front rows the people were turning round. He left the platform and moved forward quickly in the direction in which the crowd was pushing. He had to elude his colleagues' solicitous hands and even the grip of the third secretaries who tried to stop him. My scarlet robe, he thought, might protect me. My God, my crucified God, will perhaps protect me. So many breaths were all at once upon him, so many touching hands, so many white eyeballs, so many noises combined in one great buzz. He pressed forward to where the bull had come to a standstill, fifteen yards from the truculent crowd.

Tokkie Nel switched off the ignition of his truck. The bull pawed the ground, shoved angrily at the wreck of a car, swung round towards Tokkie, and then back towards the crowd. When the farmer looked round he saw that his workers had beaten a retreat and were already half-way back to the Casspirs. Slowly he climbed out, never taking his eyes off the crowd. Cautiously, he closed on the bull, holding his hat in his hand, as if to say: I come in peace. In the other hand he held the short bullhook with which he had to hook the bull's nose-ring if he was to lead him back to the truck.

The bishop was half-way through the crowd, his scarlet robe already trampled awry and grubby, stained with saliva and sweat stains, when the bull decided it was preferable to take on the faceless masses than the single man who advanced on him so purposefully. The bishop could hear the officers warning over the loudhailers: 'Sir, turn round at once. Sir, turn round at once. You are creating a security risk. We repeat: you are creating a security risk.' Are they talking to me? wondered the bishop for a moment, and then realised: someone was approaching the crowd. Around him the fists were raised ever higher, and at once he could see, over the bobbing heads and through the dust, the bull charging into the crowd.

Miraculously the crowd parted before the charge and the raking horns caught no one. Then, with a dread that suddenly became part of his body, the bishop saw Tokkie Nel jogging after the bull. And behind the farmer, three Casspirs that had broken away from the formation and were slowly easing forward. Muttering to himself, the bishop pressed forward, lost sight of bull and man, saw only heads, hands, elbows, gaping mouths. Once he was knocked to the ground and someone trod on his cheek, his cross was wrenched from his neck and landed in the dust at his feet. No more blood, he prayed against the background of the crowd's chants, just no more blood.

When Tokkie Nel realised that his bull had gone irrecoverably into the crowd, he wanted to turn round and run back to his truck, but it was already too late. He was surrounded by people who tossed him from outstretched hand to outstretched hand. He fell once, but came upright again through sheer brute strength, lost his hat and bullhook, his watch was torn from his arm and he saw the jiggling red uvula of a woman as she screamed in his face. She pressed herself against him and he shoved her away madly. Strange, he thought in an instant when time froze, I don't have any final thoughts. I am frozen in a calm panic.

The bull had cleared a small arena for himself within the crowd. He staggered round, crazed by rage and fear, and two home-made knives had already been thrust into his hump. Blood streaked his flanks. The crowd goaded him and stones smacked against his back. One struck him in the eye and blinded him temporarily.

The bishop saw the crowd milling round the bull, but he tried to push through to where Tokkie was being thrown about. Once he saw the farmer's hair bobbing above the crowds, then a white hand and a forearm like those of a drowning man. Praying, he thrust forward. Later he began to scream. Perhaps he should have stayed at the microphone: he had more power there.

Then, bloodied and tattered, the white man was thrown into the arena.

Tokkie Nel was on hands and knees in front of the bull. He saw the knives in the hump and he saw the blood streaks and the blind eye. He tried to stand up but a flying stone caught him on the leg. The bull charged him but was also struck with a stone, swung away, foaming at the mouth. Farmer Tokkie stared at the circle of feet round him. Everyone has feet, the thought flashed through his mind. So many feet. Just look at the feet. He looked up just as the bishop, with a massive expenditure of energy, managed to shove himself into the front line. Tokkie took in the bishop's tattered scarlet robe. It's one of those communist priests, was his last thought before he lost consciousness.

The bishop had to summon his last ounce of courage to step into the ring. He saw the bull aiming at him and thought: What a blessing it would be to die at those horns rather than at the hands of this crowd. But he thought no further. He stepped forward and stood beside Tokkie. A stone struck him in the back, he nearly fell forward, he saw a car tyre passed over the heads of the crowd, he smelt petrol through the dust. He glanced at the farmer lying unconscious at his feet. Then he raised his arms and yelled with all the rage and frustration of his authority, all the fear in his body, all the faith that he could summon up: 'No!'

And again 'No!'

And once again when another stone struck him, 'No!'

The bull was still aiming at him. The bishop looked into the bull's dark eye and he saw the anger and fear. He saw the bull's breath pumping through its nostrils. He stepped forward over the prone farmer. He walked slowly, step by step, with outstretched arms to the bull. He kept his eyes on the bull's dark eye. The crowd became quieter. A last stone fell next to the bishop. The nose-ring, he thought, I must get hold of the nose-ring.

As the hubbub around him subsided and he moved forward step by step, he thought: Perhaps, after all, I am wearing the right uniform.

Bull Factory

The fastest gun in town, you're up front. Leading the field.

The crowd follows. You set the pace.

But success has a price tag. Peak performance takes its toll.

In love you've got to be number one.

Naturally: you're a top dog.

We understand.

That's why we've taken an old recipe, proved by lovers down the ages. And in our laboratories we have developed it into NEW Don Juan ointment.

I drew a deep breath and read on.

Don Juan ointment will put the bang back in your love-life! Shoot you through to total pleasure!

The creative director pressed a button and the bottom of an ointment tin flashed onto the projection screen: *Don Juan: tested in San Francisco, sex-mecca of the world. The secret of movie stars who stay on top in spite of great pressure and tension. Heroes of the silver screen who go for the bull's-eye every time!*

Guaranteed safe and free from side-effects for you or your lover! Order now from Venus Products, PO Box 3386, Bellville Industria. And receive a FREE surprise gift from Loveland with your first tin of success ointment!

The MD's cigar tapped against the gold-plated ashtray. He watched Big Bill van Niekerk out of the corner of his eye, keeping the other eye critically fixed on my presentation, from market analysis to concept and media plan. I pushed my seat back, signalled to the creative director and the logo which we'd created flashed onto the screen. I read the slogan once, twice, three times; first quietly, then louder, then emphatically: *Venus – won't let you down.*

Big Bill started to laugh. He chuckled and chortled and guffawed. Unsure, we sat in the gloom. The MD shifted uncomfortably. The creative director mopped his brow. Just the week before he'd blown a big pitch. He was living on borrowed time: the Afro, the Pierre Cardin shirt, the jeans and the silver neckchain didn't quite disguise the fact that he was pushing 40. In this game, over the hill.

While Big Bill laughed, the MD gestured to the secretary. She laid the written proposal, elegantly bound in gold, before Big Bill, accidentally brushing against his shoulder as she did so.

I flashed back to my first meeting with him, the day he'd come to brief us about yet another new product.

'So, you're the new account executive,' he'd said, and as he thrust a warm paw in my direction he was already looking over my shoulder at what we'd laid on for him in the MD's office: a wooden box of his favourite cigars (standard equipment for every advertising agency pitching for Big Bill's accounts), a brace of chic little female media assistants draped around the table and a bottle of the KWV's finest brandy.

'We must get together for a drink tomorrow,' he'd said, pushing past me. 'You can pay. Where the fuck is that secretary of mine? She's all tits and no brains. Come on, Hilary baby, let's get going. I've only got seven minutes.'

We sat. I couldn't help assessing Big Bill's monumental paunch which rose and fell heavily as he breathed. His coarse fingers were heavily weighted with rings. Big Bill's Hilary noted down every word he uttered.

'Right, it's bloody straightforward,' he'd bellowed, 'but it's dynamite. I believe in it and I'm ready to fight for it. I'm giving it to you because this is a young agency, you run with a campaign, and you're randy buggers. You've got the account, but I'm only giving you one chance at a media splash and if it doesn't take first shot, you're on your arses on the street.'

We'd nodded. We all knew Big Bill's war-cry: 'I carry a helluva lot of weight in this city.'

'Fair enough,' said the MD, tapping his cigar on the gold-plated ashtray.

There'd been a moment's silence. Then, 'Here it is,' said Big Bill, and Hilary produced a small bottle from her brief-case. We'd waited in anticipation as Hilary solemnly unscrewed the lid and handed the bottle to Big Bill.

He stuck a fat pinkie into the ointment and held it out to the MD.

'Careful, girls,' he'd teased.

We'd all sniffed the pink ointment and nodded approvingly.

'This is IT,' pronounced Big Bill, tossing back the rest of his brandy. The MD flicked his lighter as Big Bill's hand moved towards the cigar box.

'Hell, boys,' said Big Bill through clouds of smoke. 'You've got to give this thing one helluva name, because it's a knockout product. Supermarkets, cafés – these are the distribution points. Cafés, man. That's where you must push it. Along with bread, Blitz, *Scope* and the Sunday paper. This is a Sunday game: they've got air-conditioning, they've got slim-fasters, they've got aerobouncy mattresses, they've got vibrators. What they need now is the performance. And there you have it. There it is.' Big Bill had tapped the bottle. We nodded: no one in this town argued with Big Bill's marketing savvy.

'We're gonna take the suburbs by storm with this product,' bellowed Big Bill.

Filthy rich, with a liver beyond the rescue of any health farm, this was a man who'd gone into liquidation four times, and every time bounced back with a new Alfa

Spider, driving from agency to agency with a new wonder product.

'Media?' The MD raised an enquiring eyebrow.

'TV,' said Big Bill. 'We go big.'

'The SABC will never approve it,' cautioned the MD.

'You're the agency,' said Big Bill. 'What does it say out there in reception? "We sell ice to Eskimos." Come on, man.' He'd stubbed out his cigar. 'This is your game. Chuck it at your best studio and see what they come up with. And have a look at the competition. I want a market analysis. And you present within a week. Agreed?'

He stood up while Hilary scribbled down his last words. Their car, a company BMW, was already idling at the door. It sank down on its axles as Big Bill climbed into the back.

Back inside, the MD had drawn a deep breath and pushed the blond forelock back off his forehead.

'Bastard,' he'd said, and then, to the receptionist: 'Set up a meeting, seven tonight in my office. This is a biggie.'

Now, four days later, we sat limply in the presentation room waiting for Big Bill's stomach convulsions to subside. What was the verdict?

Finally, he looked up and announced: 'I know a campaign when I see one!' The MD's cigar flew to his mouth, the creative director whistled softly.

'For fucksakes,' I heard him mutter.

'Talk about market penetration!' gloated Big Bill. The MD made a small movement with his head and a fresh brandy appeared before Big Bill.

I sighed too. Three hard days had followed that first brainstorming session at the round table from 7 p.m. on the Monday. We'd started tired and tense after a long and exhausting day and broken up the meeting half drunk and irritable. For one whole day a researcher had called every gynaecologist, quack, muti shop, pharmacist and analyst. The next day she explored every nook and cranny of the city, and finally, with the campaign that gradually crystallised from the chaos of sketches and photos and words, she produced a neatly typed list of aphrodisiacs and sex aids. They were all there, from countless mixtures of Spanish fly to indigenous rhino-horn powders, passion fruit cordials from the French Riviera, witchdoctors' mutis and potions from the Bo-Kaap. And a row of pink pills from Woodstock's drug belt. The minute we had the list we were up and running.

It was already 1 a.m. by the time we started the night-club round, tired but enthusiastic. I got stuck in a joint with a saxophone player and a blind clown; the others went off somewhere to gamble with the cast of Marthinus Basson's new production. Next morning I heard that the MD, exhausted and drained to the dregs by cars, perfume, brandy, Bible courses, short-term insurance and chewing-gum, had started folding R50-notes into little pink aeroplanes which he sent flying round the club. The chronically broke actors scurried like fowls after the little planes, fawned on him, applauded him and hated him with his paunch and his heavy gold signet ring.

And now, with Big Bill lyrical, it was an evening of relaxation.

'I know a campaign when I see one,' chortled Big Bill again. Then he leaned over to say something to the MD. I caught the creative director's eye. Behind his relief, I could see the exhaustion of twenty years in the bull factory. Later he excused himself; he was off to the Big Wheel, where the men sat for hours drinking beer, eating German sausages and giving the come-on to each other's reflections in the mirrors.

As he left, he cried over our jollity the cry that always signalled he was fucked-out: 'I'm bisexual: I love men *and* boys!'

'Goodbye, Arthur Murray,' said the MD. The man in

jeans had earned his spurs again. We had Big Bill in the bag.

The MD glanced at his watch. Seven o'clock. 'What about an early night?' The PAs and secretaries made a happy and chattering bee-line for the door. Shortly afterwards a couple of AEs followed them, each with a file under one arm, briefcase in the other hand. Silence fell in the palace. So there we were: the MD, Big Bill, Hilary, the copywriter, the media director and I.

We sat in the blue haze of cigar smoke, waiting until the last door banged. We charged our glasses. Big Bill fidgeted restlessly: he wanted his pound of flesh. Earlier, a messenger had deposited an *Argus* on the MD's desk. Now the MD drew it nearer, running a finger down the smalls. He dialled. The gold ring gleamed in the low light.

While we waited, I had to move Big Bill's Spider from the kerb in front of the office to our parking garage. He'd refused to allow a messenger to do it.

'If you want to handle my account,' he growled at me, 'you'd better learn to handle my Spider. Some days I have a gut full of driving.'

In the luxury car, I recalled what the tired art director had said to me the evening before: 'It pays to cut your ear off.'

At the same time, the English copywriter had pushed his typewriter back and leaned over to me. I could smell stale brandy on his breath.

'When the pupil is ready,' he murmured, 'the master will arrive...'

'Zola shits,' was how I'd shut him up and left. Behind me jazz blared from the loudspeakers. They were under a lot of pressure. I'd brought a bottle of Nederburg Baronne up to the studio for them; there was the crazy aroma of dagga and the copywriter's head was slouched forward on his arms.

With Big Bill's Spider safe beside the MD's BMW, I made

my way up the stairs from the basement garage. I stopped at the toilet on one floor. Above the urinal, someone had written in koki pen: *Enjoy the last great white erection*. And alongside: *Aids rules OK*. Someone had crossed out the *Aids* and replaced it with *PW*. On the floor below ours, I greeted the security guard and his fierce Alsatian with its shifty eyes.

At our office, I rang the doorbell.

The intercom crackled. 'Yes?' It was the MD.

'Yup.'

The electronic Yale sprang open. I entered. A bunch of red poppies on a chrome and glass table. Fallen petals lay on the glass. Aha, I thought: the Sanlam ad.

The girls hadn't arrived yet. Big Bill was telling his favourite story: about the Ciskeian mama who'd been bribed into having a minute microphone implanted behind one nipple so she ... Big Bill was in paroxysms of laughter. So that at night she could milk the Minister of Development for information on new transactions. 'Via that big mama's left tit,' said Big Bill, 'I made my first million.'

I sat down and poured more wine. For Big Bill's entertainment, the media director went to the Big Bill file drawer, took out a video and slipped it into the VCR. Bored, we watched a girl with a briefcase enter an office block, ride up in the lift, walk down a corridor, knock on a door and enter. With a nod, she acknowledged the man behind the large desk, put her briefcase down, and began to strip. The man bent over his intercom and, when she was naked, three young men came into the office. They stripped too and the man at the desk relaxed back in his chair and watched the panting performance.

'And Hilary?' I whispered to the media director. He frowned and shook his head.

'She stays,' he mouthed. Sitting next to Big Bill, Hilary watched the video with interest. She giggled at one point and asked me to pour her another drink.

We all prayed that it wasn't to be a night for Big Bill's most enduring passion: kerb crawling: the long convoy led by Big Bill's Spider and the MD's BMW, creeping along Sea Point's main road, Woodstock's main road, down Loop Street ... for hours on end: Big Bill in the leading car, filthy rich, *almost* a member of the President's Council, red-faced, blustering.

At last the doorbell rang. The MD looked at me. As I went out, the girl on the video shrieked something ecstatically in Italian.

'Mamma mia!' groaned Big Bill.

It was late night, in fact early morning – one could tell by the subtle change in the drone of the city – when I cautiously opened the door. In an elderly Ford Cortina slung low on its axles, I saw white female elbows, a wrist smothered in bangles. The man before me sported a droopy cowboy moustache. His pants hung low on his pelvis. In a comic replication of a Hollywood movie, a revolver occupied the holster on his hip.

'You phoned Thrill Girls?' he asked.

I nodded. 'Let's go in.'

I made sure the door was latched. I could hear the girls tittering in the Cortina. We moved through the dimly-lit entrance foyer, on deep-pile carpets, past the glossy wall-posters, manicured indoor plants; past framed Loerie Awards, logos, glossy pictures of models, a cheetah posing on a locomotive, a spacecraft splashing down in a blue sea, a giant hot-air balloon with an entire city in its belly. The ape following me slid his eyes over glass and chrome, gleaming desks behind transparent partitions, designer vases with fresh roses, the blank gaze of computer monitors, and past the studios: the colourful roosts of the visualisers, copywriters and artists.

'Go for the gold,' he read in a murmur and a sceptical

laugh stirred the moustache.

'Capitalism gives everyone a chance,' I told him sarcastically.

'Plenty bucks here,' he said and whistled softly. We turned a corner in the corridor. Before us, through the open door, lay the arresting elegance of the MD's suite.

I heard Big Bill's snigger. He was telling yet another well-known story: about the milk culture chaps from the North, already driving a flashy car seven years ago, who had come to him for backing.

'And now,' Big Bill threw out an arm, 'look at the buggers queueing up there in Loop Street in front of TeKaibos. Look at the big Mercs from the platteland. There are fat cats in that queue, pal. And now I hear even the fucking English are starting to buy.'

We entered the room. The MD tapped his cigar against his cheek.

'What have you got for me?' he asked the cowboy.

'My agency fee is only fifty a head. Beyond that you must negotiate.' He fingered his holster.

'Why so cheap?' asked the MD. He had a few under the belt and I could tell he was spoiling for an argument.

The cowboy-pimp stepped forward and extended a hand to the MD. 'Alcock,' he introduced himself.

'What cock?' quipped Big Bill and Hilary's giggle tinkled round the room. On the video – the sound had been turned down – the girl with the briefcase once more walked down the corridor and knocked at the door. Without a word, she nodded to the man at the desk and he bent over his intercom. She unhooked her bra and her breasts fell out. Three men came into the room. The man at the desk relaxed into his chair.

The MD raised an eyebrow at the creative director, who speedily topped up Big Bill's glass – three fingers of brandy this time. The sooner we had him paralytic, the sooner we could get him out. Hilary crossed her legs and I imagined I heard the sound of silky stockings rubbing against each other.

'Fuck the protocol,' said the MD, ignoring Alcock's outstretched hand. 'What have you got?'

'Two blondes, a redhead and three brunettes. The brunettes are all Spanish. And clean. All checked this evening. Safe like mommy.'

The MD looked sideways at Alcock. The ash at the end of his cigar was longer than usual. 'And the piece?' he asked without allowing his eyes to move to the revolver.

'The city's getting rough,' Alcock shrugged.

'The Cape isn't Dutch any more,' smirked Big Bill; then, with an expansive gesture: 'Bring in the follies!'

Alcock turned to Big Bill.

The MD looked at Alcock. 'That fellow', he said, 'is one of the heaviest of the Cape's heavies.'

Big Bill giggled. 'Wild Bill,' he bragged, redder in the face than ever.

'Fine. My girls are experienced.'

'If I touch something,' began Big Bill, rising out of his chair. Alcock looked slightly nervous as Bill drew himself up to his full height. 'If I get hold of something, it turns to gold. Even if I get hold of a girl's tits.' He winked at Hilary who got a fresh cigar out of the case for him.

'As long as your cheques are healthy,' said Alcock.

'I own the fucking bank. The whole fucking bank.' Big Bill was a bit unsteady on his feet.

'How much?' asked the MD, signing a cheque with a flourish. He looked at Hilary; the first time he'd looked directly at her or spoken to her. 'Are you sticking around or fading?'

She simpered, 'My job is my job.'

'Deliver,' the MD told Alcock, waving his hand like an orchestra conductor. He threw himself back in his chair. We waited in silence. Even Big Bill said nothing as he fixed his eyes on the video screen.

Outside we heard a car. The MD glanced at his watch.

We could hear them coming down the corridor, their high heels whispering on the wool matting. I could imagine their eyes darting about for booty to filch later when the men were docile and drunk.

Even before they came through the door we could smell the sharp sweet stench of the spermicide which they'd sprayed into their slippery orifices.

'If there's one thing I hate,' said the MD as they entered, 'it's that smell.'

Even when the girls were standing before us, Big Bill kept his eyes on the video screen. The MD lit another cigar and scrutinised each of the girls in turn.

Ill at ease, I poured more wine into my glass. The media director was gazing fixedly at the blonde third from the left. He smiled at her. She winked back but then returned her gaze to the MD who was gesturing to Alcock. 'Delivery accepted,' said the MD looking at me. I escorted Alcock to the front door.

'Grab the little blonde for yourself,' he told me. 'She's double-jointed.'

When I got back to the office, a redhead had taken the seat beside mine. She smiled at me.

I poured her a glass of wine and topped mine up.

Big Bill, Hilary and their three girls were ushered to the presentation studio with its soundproof walls and deep-pile carpets. The MD went along to show them how to open the stinkwood bar cabinet and where the small video screen was concealed – behind a framed Loerie that swung aside at the touch of a button. In one hand Big Bill held the video cassette of the Italian girl, with the other he waved at us.

I followed the redhead to the promotion studio. She

wore a shiny black blouse and tight jeans and she swayed her hips as she went up the stairs in front of me. I heard the MD's door shut with a bang, and jazz was already spinning from the wine studio – Brubeck's *Give it all ya got*, the copywriter's favourite.

I closed the door to the promotion studio. A big chrome robot under construction for an oil company's careers exhibition gleamed electronically in the corner. They'd forgotten to switch it off. I pulled out the wall plug, the eyes flickered, the robot sighed, shuddered and went dead.

I sat down.

She was not unattractive: gingery hair, rather heavy mascara, freckles on her nose. She paced coquettishly about the studio, leaning over half-finished sketches, smiling at the posters. Outside, far away, a siren wailed. Then it fell silent again. Slowly the city subsided into its late-night sleep.

She came to sit opposite me so that our shoes touched. In the curve of her neck, where the blouse fell open, there was a bluegreen bruise. She leant forward towards me, her elbows on her thighs.

'The night is still young, hmm?'

I nodded and poured us each a drink. She read the label on the bottle and pursed her lips. 'Nothing but the best, hey?' I shrugged. We heard a door slam somewhere. Heels tapping on the marble floor of the toilet. Another slam, voices. A telephone began to ring deep in the belly of the firm. We heard it ring ten, twenty times.

'Hard day?' she asked.

'I can't remember,' I said, taking another mouthful of wine.

'When did you start this morning?'

'Clock-watching is a cardinal sin.'

'Oh.' She shrugged as if to say sorry-I-asked and looked around the room again. Would she get up and walk about, running her finger over the sleeping icons of the bull factory?

But she remained seated, and I did too, with tie awry and waistcoat unbuttoned. Then she remembered her strategy. She pouted, pulled her shoulders back and aimed her nipples provocatively at me.

'Cigarette?' she asked. I nodded. She snapped her small handbag open, holding it pressed intimately against herself as she delved about in it. What did she keep in there? Condoms? Tissues? Vaseline?

I took a cigarette from the red-nailed fingers. Dagga? A sanitary pad?

We lit up and drew on the cigarettes. A set of red underwear, should the client require it? A little apron, should the client desire that?

She watched me awhile through the smoke. Then, 'You don't like me,' she complained with a pout.

I shifted on my stool.

'What are your rates?' I asked.

She looked at me for a long moment. 'I've had my tits done recently,' she said. Fixing her eyes on mine, she slowly unbuttoned her blouse. One breast appeared: full and curved, perfect. Then the other nipple slipped out. She had large breasts, round as melons, and the nipples pointed pertly upwards from rosy stains the size of your palm.

She pushed one breast sideways. 'See the marks?' The flesh swelled out from her hand, thrusting through between the fingers. She left the full breast; it swayed dizzyingly back.

We sat; smoked.

Behind her on the wall, the copywriter who normally worked here had pinned up a passage from Ogilvy:

"I always use my clients' products. This is not toadyism, but elementary good manners. Almost everything I consume is manufactured by one of my clients. My shirts are by Hathaway, my candlesticks by Steuben. My car is a Rolls-Royce and its tank is always full of Shell. I have my suits made by Sears, Roebuck. At breakfast I drink Maxwell House coffee or Tetley Tea, and eat two slices of Pepperidge Farm toast. I wash with Dove, deodorize with Ban, and light my pipe with a Zippo lighter … and why not, pray tell? Are these not the finest goods and services on earth?"

She stood up and started to peal off her jeans. They were very tight, and she had to wiggle her hips. She folded the jeans neatly over the artist's drawing table. Then she took off her panties, tossing them onto the jeans.

I poured more wine. There was a smudge of red lipstick on her glass. She sat before me again. Her pubic hair was rusty red, growing lustily in a single tuft from just below the sunburn mark, halfway to the navel. She'd shaved the inside of her thighs and new growth was showing from under the skin. I lit two more cigarettes and gave her one. She ran red fingernails across her lips. Then she began to rub herself, and I could hear the sound of her hand against the wiry hairs. Moaning softly, she put her cigarette in the ashtray and massaged her left nipple. I drew on my cigarette, taking a mouthful of wine now and then. I could smell her now.

When she came, I heard the swishing of the big yellow machine that moves along the city's kerbstones, sucking up refuse from four o'clock each morning. In the little death she sat before me, her body jerking, her mournful eyes on me, her mouth a crushed, sorrowing flower of the night.

Faces

He came into town from the north. First there were smallholdings on either side of the road, with patches of wilted lucerne, limp mealies, an old man hoeing, drunk with the sun and the toil.

Then the commercial premises. A sign announced briefly: *Hotel Bar Whites*. A few metres further on, with a gaggle of drinkers in front of it: *Bar Coloureds*. He drove on, suppressing the desire for a long cold beer. Past the service station and the General Dealer. It was sweltering and godforsaken. The eyes of the people on the pavements fell eagerly on his numberplate. He came from far away, beyond the horizon; the place from where the telephone poles came striping rhythmically over the hills.

He stopped at a hardware shop that sold farm implements. He asked a man sitting on a plough, 'Where's the police station?'

The man explained, down *that* way then *that* way. 'You'll see the sign.'

He drew up and got out at the police station. It was hot. He put on his jacket and pulled a comb through his hair. Wiped the worst of the sweat from his eyes and his brow. He took the old briefcase from the boot, and his footsteps crunched over the gravel under the pepper trees. Yellow-faced convicts sitting in the shade greeted him as he passed them. They were checking him over, he knew – his shoes, his jacket, his car. They looked at his briefcase and the ring on his finger.

He entered the cool charge office. At first there didn't

seem to be anyone in there. Then he saw an old sergeant behind a stack of files.

'Good-day, sarge,' he greeted him, taking off his sunglasses politely. In these small towns, people wanted to look into you. They didn't like things to be hidden away. They wanted to have a good look at everything, turning it over in the mind and savouring it for gossip on the stoeps of the town later. He knew these small towns only too well. Their hotels, their charge offices, their widows, their young farmers with brains addled by the sun, dicing through town in their Datsun bakkies, a packet of Lexington in the shirt pocket, a 303 rifle on the passenger seat and a youngster on the back to open gates.

The sergeant didn't look up. He was obviously going to finish filling in his form first. All right then, he would begin to unpack. He put his briefcase on the counter. The catches sprang open. There were stacks of photographs inside. Hundreds of faces gazed up at him. How he hated them and the dead gloss of their smiles. The backwardness that lay shallow in their eyes. Stupid, a little bit too stupid, with a morose twist at the corners of the mouth, typical platteland.

He took them out, first the twenty-by-twenties, then the bigger ones, the thirty-by-thirties. There were also a couple that were postcard-size. He made three stacks and wiped the sweat from his forehead. Then he put the briefcase down on the floor again. Cleared his throat.

The sergeant looked up. 'MorningSargePretoorscanhelp?' It came out slurred into one word.

He nodded, because he couldn't find the energy to speak. But then remembered: friendliness. 'Please, sarge.'

The sergeant approached, bulging out of his uniform. He looked at the photos suspiciously. 'Yes?'

'I'm sure you know all your people around here, sarge.'

'Yes?'

Outside someone was yelling at the convicts. The metallic slam of a police-van door. Many feet on the gravel.

'Twenty years on this beat,' said the sergeant.

'I just want to know if you recognise any of these faces.'

The sergeant looked at him suspiciously. 'Who are these people, mister? Are you a journalist?'

'No, I'm not from the newspaper. Tois Greeff, freelance photographer.' He indicated his car outside, as though it would lend weight to his claim. The sergeant leaned over and noted the strange numberplate.

'Oh,' he said.

He showed the pictures to the sergeant one at a time. Starting with the big ones. The old widow first of all. He remembered her sitting-room with the china and coloured feathers in a display cabinet. Her old-woman's ankles so fat they hung over her shoes.

'You must touch out the liver spots, dearie,' she'd said.

He remembered the framed pictures of the Battle of Blood River and the Voortrekker Monument, the smell of the Aga range in the kitchen, the tinkle of teaspoons against cups, but he could not remember the town.

The Lord knew, the one town was just like another. One old woman just like another.

He would knock at a front door, having parked his car so they could see the numberplate. He had his card ready in case anyone opened up. On it was printed in fancy type *Tois J Greeff Freelance Photographer Portrait Studies Family Groups Baby Pictures Christening and Wedding Ceremonies 3 Station Road Kraaifontein (near Cape Town) Glossy or Matt.*

The sergeant studied the widow for a long time. Then he said, 'Not from these parts. She looks like one of the Swarts from Porterville way. People say they have Jewish blood. You can see it in her widow's peak. And her bottom lip. Greedy old woman, you can tell.'

Greeff made a note. Porterville. A day's drive away.

'That's a great help, sarge. A great help.'

'And this one?'

The photo was of a shrivelled old couple looking for all the world as if they were already dead. Like the mealies on the outskirts of town, he thought. They were sitting in front of the backcloth he always hung up for his portraits. It showed a waterfall, a wide road, a flock of birds and heavenly light radiating out above the heads of the subjects. Tucked away somewhere was a young shepherd with a crook. And at the bottom right: *Tois J Greeff, portrait studies.*

The sergeant scrutinised the old couple. 'They look sick,' he said. 'Not from round here. Try more to the northwest. Look how dried out the old man is.' A quiet laugh rumbled deep in his paunch.

To the northwest. Could the world be so flat? A tortoise had come slowly closer when he'd stopped to relieve himself against a thorn tree. Then the tortoise saw the urine splash down, hissed and withdrew into its shell. It lay there like a stone for ages. Then it had stumbled off. Greeff had fastened his fly and gone back to the car. He'd driven on, trailing his long tail of dust.

'I've just come from the northwest, sergeant. These two live somewhere else.'

The sergeant looked up. 'Why don't you keep the addresses, son?'

Greeff met the old sergeant's eyes. Then he took a third picture. Studied it: a fat baby, laughing, with chubby hands.

'The world is a big place,' he said. He examined his fingernails. 'And full of misunderstandings.'

'That's a fact,' said the sergeant. 'The drought carries on even though they pray for rain every Sunday. It hasn't rained since the year before last. You should see how the stock is dying out to the west.' The sergeant sighed. 'Why don't you try at Welfare?'

They'd been through all the photos. The sergeant had recognised two faces. One was a salesman at the hardware shop. The other a girl who'd worked at the exchange, but she'd moved on. To the city. Greeff made his notes. He put everything away and snapped the catches on the briefcase. They said goodbye.

'Good luck, son,' said the sergeant.

'Thanks, sarge. Thanks for your help.'

'You must find the other people, son.'

'I'll get them, sergeant. I'll get them.'

'That's money you've got in that briefcase, son.'

'That's right, sarge. It's money. There's money in photos.'

The sergeant's laugh rumbled in his stomach again. 'Only if you can find the faces.'

'As long as you get them, sarge. As long as you get them.'

Greeff raised a hand. 'Just say the word if I can fix you up with a photo. Maybe in uniform?'

'Yes, yes, when I retire, son. Next year, maybe then. Of me and the wife. Just for one last time in the uniform of the Force.'

'That's right, sarge, I'll take it. For nothing, in return for your help with the photos.'

'Okay, son. Drive safely.'

He left. Crunching along the gravel under the pepper trees. The convicts were gone. A colourful rooster scratched about near the front wheel of the car. Splashes showed that dogs had also been round the car.

He put the briefcase in the boot and drove off.

At the hardware shop he stopped. The man was still sitting on the plough. Yes, it was definitely the same one. Greeff got out, smiling now.

'Sir,' he said, approaching him. The man stood up.

'Did you find the police station?' he asked.

'Yes, yes, thanks. Your directions were good. Don't you remember me?'

The man looked at him, then at the car.

'Search me,' he said.

'Greeff, Tois J. Greeff. Freelance photographer.'

'Oh yes?' The man was still at a loss.

'I have a surprise for you.'

'Oh?' Then the man realised he hadn't introduced himself. His surname was Burger.

Greeff unlocked the boot. He took out the briefcase. Sitting on the plough, he snapped the catches open. Burger whistled quietly. Then it all came back to him. 'Well, I'll be buggered. I'll be buggered. Yessirree, that's me.' He was pleased now. 'This is a surprise, man. Nothing much happens round here, you know.' He lit a cigarette and studied the photo critically. 'With a tie on, too, hey.'

Greeff grinned. 'I've had a job tracking you down. The sergeant helped me.'

'That old jackal. He knows everyone. Hell, man, what do I owe you?'

'Three rand seventy-eight.'

'I'll have to draw some money. Come with me and we can sink a couple of beers. Hell, what a surprise.

'Well, I'll be buggered,' he said as they walked away from Greeff's car. 'And you've come such a long way.' He looked at Greeff's numberplate and shook his head.

Would he ever forget the first time the messenger of the court had arrived with the summons? Martha was still in bed, her Saturday morning lie-in, with the green curlers in her hair. She was reading the newspaper, the property guide. She wanted to move from Kraaifontein to Durbanville. Or to that impossible dream: the hills of Welgemoed.

'Mr Greeff?' the messenger had asked.

'That's right.'

'Matthys Johannes Greeff?'

'That's right. Yes?'

'I am the messenger of the court. I have been instructed to attach your possessions.'

'My possessions?'

'Yes, all moveable property.'

'Like?'

'Your moveable assets.'

'What for? Who do I owe money to?'

'The creditor is Photofast Enterprises.'

'What for?'

Martha had joined them by now, without the property guide.

'The debt was incurred by ...' The messenger checked his papers ... 'Yes, goods bought and delivered at your request and on your authority.'

'Goods?'

Martha chipped in, 'Yes, the darkroom equipment, the long lens. Didn't you pay for them? He said he'd paid. I even asked. What do we do now?'

As they stood arguing, the messenger slipped past them, into the house. He listed everything.

'And now?' Greeff asked when he was finished.

'You can still pay,' said the messenger. 'If you pay quickly, we won't remove the things.'

'And if I don't pay?'

'Then we take the things and sell them by public auction.'

'My things?'

'We have attached your possessions, Mr Greeff, you must not remove anything from these premises.'

'But are they still our things?' asked Martha.

She was crying now.

'You must ask your lawyer,' said the messenger. 'I am only doing my job. I only make the list.'

'But are they still our things?' sobbed Martha. 'Our things? Our things?'

Greeff jerked back to the present when Burger said beside him, 'Another beer, old man? Another Amstel?'

'No,' said Greeff. 'A brandy. A double.'

'This one's on me,' said Burger. 'Can you believe it? I'll be buggered. I'll be buggered.'

'Do you know this part of the world?' asked Greeff.

'Grew up here,' Burger answered.

'And the people?'

'Know them well, man. Very well. Every face.'

'Could you help me with my photos?'

'Sure, man. Let's go back to the shop and have a look there.'

'Are they still our things?' Martha had asked. 'Our things?'

'I'll have to ask a lawyer.'

'Then he'll want to be paid. We haven't got money.'

God, life was a bankrupt business. So many faces in one case. All the faces; how well he knew them all.

'Face-pedlar,' he told Burger. 'I'm a bloody face-pedlar.'

'Come on, old man,' said Burger, 'Cheer up. Cheer up.'

'I'm a bloody face-pedlar.'

'So what? I'm a plough pedlar.'

'Faces and ploughs. Why can't we be rich too? Look at that fat cat in his fancy car.'

'I know him,' said Burger. 'Coetzee of Grootfontein. You should see his debts. Everything on account, including his Mercedes. Even his wife.' He laughed.

'Bloody face-pedlar.'

He'd rang a lawyer. Asked.

'Come and see me.'

'What do you charge?'

'For a consultation?'

'Yes.'

'Well, that depends. Do you need advice or defence?'

'I don't know.'

'Do you want to enter a plea for defence?'

'Against what?' he asked. 'They've made a list of my things.'

'Then it's too late,' the lawyer told him. 'You should have come a long time ago.'

'But what will you charge if I come to see you?'

'That depends,' said the lawyer. 'I am free on Wednesday afternoon.'

'That suits me.'

He never went.

He and Burger had gone through the briefcase. 'A couple of good-looking chicks,' said Burger. 'You must shape out quite well on the road.' He waited avidly.

'Yes,' said Greeff. 'Specially with the widows.'

'Young ones?' asked Burger.

'They're all looking for a bit of love.'

'Hey,' said Burger. 'Hey, you lucky swine. Bloody hell, I'll be buggered. I'll be buggered.'

'You can say that again,' Greeff told him. 'When they spot a foreign body, it's open season. First, you hang up your background cloth. You know: full of lights and sheep and waterfalls and stuff like that. By then they're already getting in the mood. Then you set up your lights, in the corners of the room. They've started to become aware of their own bodies. They ... they feel all *body*. Then they go and get dressed. Their best things. All dolled up, I tell you.'

'Sunday best,' Burger added.

'That's it. Then you get them to sit under the lights. You say they should relax a bit first. And then they get very nervous. They want to know how they look. How is the light on their faces? Is the hair all right? Are there shadows under the eyes? You say, "How about a cup of tea first while you get used to the lights and the camera. The lights aren't easy. And the camera sees everything. It captures your face and fixes it for always. You can't change back again."'

'Hey, hey, you old bugger,' said Burger.

'And then I say, "Come on, sit down and relax now." You smooth her hair. Then you kneel in front of her and touch up her eyebrows a little with your black pencil. Then you go over her mouth with the lipstick. She's on fire by now. On fire, I'm telling you. Then you get the powder and just fluff it over her cheeks, her brow. You let a little powder fall onto her frock and then you brush it off, carefully.'

'Fuck, but you're a randy bugger,' said Burger. He shifted on his seat and leaned over the brochures for ploughs and tractors.

'And then,' continued Greeff, 'you say something.'

'Like what? Like what?'

'Well, something like, "We must get that deep black in your eyes." Or: "Your full lips! They're very special: I'm going to concentrate on your lips. Relax your mouth, come on, relax those cheeks too. I think just a touch more colour on the lower lip."'

'Oh, God, you old fucker,' said Burger.

'Man, then you get her hands into the right position. And she's helpless, helpless. Putty in your hands. Then you turn the lights on her and disappear under your black cloth. And then it's just her and the lens. She's all face. That whole woman shows in the face.

'And you shoot and shoot. Quite a few. Even when the film is finished, you carry on pressing the button, getting her to sit like this, then like that. And then you're finished. "Right," you say. "These are going to be some of my best photos. I can't wait to develop them."

'And then she starts to relax, you know she's starting to unwind and she begins to notice your body again. A body from out of town, if you know what I mean.'

'You old jackal,' said Burger. 'You goat.'

'Fuck, have I screwed a lot of widows!' said Greeff.

'Hell, I'll be buggered. I'll be buggered,' said Burger.

They parted eventually. Burger had not recognised a single one of the faces.

Greeff drove off, soberness filtering out over the drunkenness. He felt dead, stone-cold sober as the earth around him. The sun burnt into his very blood, burnt out his marrow.

And then the divorce papers from Martha.

He remembered vividly.

The plaintiff claimed that the marriage had broken down irreparably and that there was no prospect of restoring normal marital relations, particularly because the defendant ...

And then she had listed his sins. A resumé of his life during the last few years.

Failed to provide for the family financially.

Stayed away at night, and when he returned, failed to inform her of where he had been.

Carried on various extra-marital affairs with parties unknown to the plaintiff.

Used alcohol to excess.

Assaulted her and the children. Which was not true. He, Tois Greeff, did not raise his hand to women and children, no matter how much he'd had to drink. She rubbed salt into the wounds. He must suffer.

He thought about the previous town. There was a police station but the constable who was supposed to man it had been called away to investigate a complaint in the location. The clerk of the court was the only one there and he wasn't much help.

He tried the dominee. The shepherd of this flock would surely know.

In these towns every manse was surrounded by pepper trees, each one had kudu horns hanging on the front stoep and the house was always large and dark behind the gauze screen on the front door.

Thousands of flies died in the fullness of their sins against this gauze. They drifted into the corners of the stoep where they lay in piles. Others buzzed their last on sticky fly-papers.

The dominee came to the door himself.

'Good-day to you, brother,' he said. 'Come in. You must be from another parish?'

Greeff summed the dominee up. Already too long in this world, disappointed that the Lord of Hope about whom he preached every Sunday never did anything for his little flock to make the hope go a bit further. He felt sorry for the dominee. A hope pedlar, he thought.

'What is your calling, brother?' asked the dominee. Greeff went out to fetch his briefcase. He snapped the catches open in the dim living-room. The dominee looked at him placidly over the rim of his cup. Then, surprised, at all the glossy faces.

'Why, brother,' he exclaimed. 'So many people!'

Lost souls, Greeff wanted to say.

'Please help me to find them, dominee,' he said. 'This is my bread and butter.'

'Why, brother,' exclaimed the dominee again, 'have you driven far with this case full of snapshots?'

'Yes, dominee, I am from Kraaifontein near Cape Town.'

'And you've come all the way here, brother, with these snapshots, from Cape Town?'

'Yes, dominee, I came here to find the faces, if you know what I mean."

Once again, teacup to the lips. 'Are you certain that these faces belong to our part of the world, brother?'

'That is what I'm trying to find out, dominee.'

'I see.' A moment's silence while the dominee studied him thoughtfully.

'Isn't it very lonely on the road, brother?'

'I am used to it, dominee. I think about faces and new angles to photograph them from. I think about all the faces in my case, dominee, and what they are doing now: Are the old ones dead? Are the babies crawling yet?'

'How long have you carried these faces around, brother?'

'For months, dominee. I began in Swellendam. It's probably more ... more than a year now. It must be about fourteen months.'

'Travelling about looking for these people, brother?'

'Yes, dominee, about fourteen or fifteen months.'

'That's a long time, brother.'

'It's quite a while, dominee.'

The dominee drained his cup. And asked, 'Are you finding them, brother?'

'In a way, dominee. More or less. Some of them are dead, some of the babies too. Some have left, gone to the Cape.'

'I see.'

'And once I'm down to a few, I'll advertise.'

'Where, brother?'

'I thought of the *Farmers' Weekly*, dominee.'

'That isn't a bad idea, brother.'

'I want everyone to get their faces back, dominee. Except those who are dead.'

'No, brother, you can't return those faces.'

The dominee sighed. A cock crowed outside.

'Tell me, brother, how many snapshots were there in the case when you left Cape Town?'

'A lot, dominee. About two hundred.'

'And how many remain?'

'I tracked down a lot, dominee. In Vredenburg, in one week, I got three. A christening ceremony and the baby's mother and father. All three in one lucky go, dominee.'

'And your own family, brother?'

Greeff began to take the photos out. 'I lost them, dominee.'

The photos were stacked on the coffee table before them.

'From an illness, brother?'

'No, dominee, from a misunderstanding.'

'Have you ever been in front of the camera? Really in front, like, of the lens?' asked the post-office clerk in Porterville.

'No,' Greeff told her, 'With dolly-birds like you in front of the lens I'm not needed there.'

'Will you take my picture for nothing?' she asked.

Greeff peered through the bars, saw the wilfulness of the young body in her dress.

'There are other ways of paying,' he said.

She laughed.

'Will you pay?' he asked.

'Depends on how much you want.'

'If I don't ask for a lot, I'll never get rich.'

'Do you want to take me in my costume?'

'Really? In your costume?'

She was fidgeting with a post-office stamp, stamping *Porterville, Porterville, Porterville* all over the place.

'I've got a tanga.'

'Oh?'

Greeff was excited now; little strokes of luck on the road made him forget about Martha and all that business. And when the post-office clerk came to his hotel room, he had to explain: he didn't have a camera any more. He was tired of lying. He said straight out: 'They sold my camera. These faces are all I have now. I am selling them, do you know any of them? Look, there are widows, farmers, shop-owners; here is a policeman, and ...'

She'd left in a hurry, with her bright red bikini. She had

really wanted a photo. Misunderstanding.

Lost through a misunderstanding.

Business had been good at first. He was a bit of a spiv, shiny car, good camera and lights. From town to town he'd taken photos, noting down the film numbers and the names in his register. And going back to Kraaifontein once a month to process everything. He'd take the prints with him on his next trip, delivering them at the correct addresses. Cash on delivery. Satisfaction guaranteed, a new photo if you didn't like the first one, Tois Greeff, freelance photographer from the Cape, pleased to meet you, sit like this, sit like that, smile like this.

How could so many faces be lost in this empty land? He had been searching for a year, more than a year.

The dominee opposite him, one question after another.

The sergeant who wanted to send him deeper into the desert.

Burger of the hardware shop, who poured one beer after another down his throat and only wanted to hear sordid stories.

The post-office clerk, all body ego, who looked upon his camera as a permanent mirror.

The dry roads, the obnoxious young farmers, the fowls, the flies.

And still no deliverance.

Greeff pulled up at a post office. The sign was rusty. It was hot, though it was nearly evening. He kept a supply of ten-cent coins in a small tin in his car. Depending on how far he was from Cape Town, he used a couple or more every day. He dialled, the number at his fingertips, a part of him.

The phone rang, too long.

But she would answer, he knew.

She picked up. 'Yes,' she said. She never said 'Yes?' with a question mark. She just said, Yes. She knew it was him.

'Martha,' he said.

'Yes, Tois.'

There was a moment's silence. He heard the lines hum between them. Darkness gathered around him, the small town held its breath.

'Don't you have the addresses for me, Martha.'

She didn't answer.

Then he said again, louder, 'Martha, I want my register.'

She didn't answer.

There was a long silence. Then he repeated, 'Martha! I love you, Martha.' He said it as he did every evening and she answered as she did every evening, 'I burnt your address book. I told you I'd burnt it.' Then she hung up. The phone went *click, click, kirrr* in his ear.

Greeff hung up the receiver. He went to his car. He got in and drove a little way further, to the sign that said *Bar Whites Come In Castle Lager*. He pulled up and sat awhile in the car. Then he got out, went to the boot and took out the briefcase. He walked into the bar. Strangers' faces. He sat at the counter and put the briefcase down in front of him.

He snapped open the catches.

The White Monkey

Fielies's wire car hardly touched ground as he skidded round the corner of the dairy. With a flashy swerve, he braked just in front of us, and while the home-made Cadillac swayed on its car-tube springs, he announced breathlessly, 'There's a huge monkey in the trap.'

Excitedly I thought about the troop of monkeys which I knew well but had only seen from a distance. At sunset each evening they came in from the river banks where they spent the day, to the avenue of pines where they slept. On Sunday afternoons, when the farmyard was quiet, they romped and chattered through the mealie fields.

'Hau, we've got him!' Tattie, who I'd been sitting talking to, did a little dance on the yard gravel.

'Come,' I ordered, snatching up my point-two-two from where it leaned against a bluegum and jogging off to the pines. Fielies fell in beside me, showing off with his wire car.

'He's got the cheek of the devil,' he sniggered, 'and kleinbaas should see him trying to sharpen his teeth against the wire netting.' Tattie put on a bit of steam when he heard that and we scrambled through the farmyard fence.

While Fielies struggled to get his car over, Tattie said, 'We can tie him to a pole and teach him to behave.'

'Like eating from a plate,' crowed Fielies.

I decided this was wishful thinking. 'Nonsense, he's a monkey and monkeys only eat off the ground. You know they don't even eat in the trees. The males have to shake the branches so everything falls out and then they pick it up from the ground. Aikona, he's an animal, just like any beast.'

The troop was a plague precisely because of their habit of shaking things down. They shook fruit from the trees and then only took the odd bite here and there, so a peach was seldom eaten down to the pip.

The trap was a new acquisition – similar to the ones set by farmers higher up in the kloof to catch baboons: a sturdy contraption of wire and welded pipes. In the far end of the cage lay a flat stone attached to a rope which ran up and along the cage's roof through a series of pulleys and kept the trap's door up. When the monkey lifted the stone to get at the bait under it, the rope ran through the pulleys and the door dropped shut behind him.

From some way away we could see the farm workers crowding round the cage. Fielies abandoned his car next to the track and we broke into a run. I saw Pa standing just to one side; he was engrossed in a conversation with Old Pyp.

'Get out the way, can't you see the kleinbaas wants to see the monkey thing.' Fielies forced a passage through the small kwedini round the cage. They made way for me. I took one look and nearly jumped out of my skin.

The monkey sat just like a child beside the rock in the cage.

His hands – they looked just like human hands with nails and everything – were clasping the rope and his eyes slid from one face to another. I moved closer, and his eyes met mine.

'Jô, he looks just like Tattie,' teased Fielies.

I didn't hear the mockery in his voice, just that the monkey looked like a person.

'On a pole, on a pole,' chanted Tattie gleefully.

No, I wanted to say, no, look at his hands and face; quite human. Old Pyp came up to me and grinned, 'Face jus' like an old Bushman, hey, kleinbaas?' He gave a hoarse little giggle and I stood back.

They closed round the cage.

'It's a bull, a bull,' squealed Fielies, 'just look, when he swings round ...'

'Give him a fright so he turns,' ordered old Pyp. 'Let's see.' Tattie was quick off the mark, bashing his hand against the cage. From their jubilation I knew the monkey had swung round.

'It's a ram, master,' said old Pyp over his shoulder.

I turned to my father, 'What are you going to do with him, Pa?'

'Lord, I don't know. It won't scare the troop away if we just catch one ... In future they'll just be wary of the cage and carry on plundering the mealies and peaches.'

'Are you ... going to shoot him?' With his glance the monkey had become human for me. And those hands, like a child's ...

'No ... no. Pyp says we must shear him and paint him white. They apparently did that years ago over the river and it worked well. He'll run to the troop and they'll run away from him. That way you can chase the whole troop away for good.'

A commotion broke out at the cage. The kwedini screamed and old Pyp swore violently.

'Voessek! Voessek!' Fielies's voice was shrill and excited.

'He's caught hold of Jock, oh *gattela*!' Tattie looked round guiltily – I'd heard him sneakily egging Jock on to bark at the monkey. We drew closer to the cause of the consternation: the monkey crouched just inside the wire netting and he had Jock's upper lip firmly in his teeth. Jock's hindquarters were trembling as he tried to kick free, but if he moved his head, his lip stretched into a beak. Jock knew he was stuck; he couldn't move and he couldn't bite through the wire. He began to yelp through his half-open mouth and his tail curled in-between his hind legs.

Then Pa took out his cigarette lighter and held its small flame near the monkey's head. The monkey let go of Jock and loped back to the rope where he sat trembling. Jock rushed off to the yard, his head down, shaking himself now and again.

'You …' Old Pyp told the monkey his fortune and began to poke at him through the wire with a reed.

'No, Pyp.' I stopped him, because the monkey seemed to have fixed its white-browed eyes on me. And the hands on the rope like a person's.

'We'll paint him,' decided Pa's voice behind me. 'Get me a sack, Fielies.' Fielies sprang into action while the others held an indaba about how to get the monkey into the sack.

'He'll be gone into the trees like lightning,' warned Tattie.

'Then the kleinbaas will fetch him down again with his gun.' I looked at my point two-two and imagined a bullet striking that little face.

Fielies came panting back, the blue-wire steering wheel of his Cadillac in one hand and a sack in the other.

They began their manoeuvres, first opening the trap door gingerly to see how the monkey would react. He sat dead still, his eyes staring fixedly in my direction.

I wished that he'd take the gap and get away into the trees. They decided to pick the cage up and shake him down towards the door.

Hands grabbed eagerly and they lifted it. The monkey chattered agitatedly – it was the first sound he'd made – and swung briefly on the rope. Then he tumbled through the door and, in a flash, Old Pyp had the sack over him.

I could see how the monkey thrashed about inside the sack, but old Pyp held fast, tying up the open end. With his strange bundle he set off to the farmyard trailed by the excited mob of kwedini. They quite forgot to set the cage to rights again.

I walked with Pa. 'It will keep the troop away for ever. It's a bit cruel, but with all the damage to the mealies and peaches we've got no choice ...'

'Will his hair ... grow again, Pa?' I asked carefully.

'Usually –' Pa was hesitating, I could hear – 'usually, I believe, the monkey pines to death. The troop flees from him because he's white but he can't understand why they run away from him.' Pa was silent for a moment. 'In the end, yes, he pines away.'

'Oh.'

I couldn't take my eyes off the thrashing sack that Old Pyp held. I imagined that the monkey's white-browed eyes were still staring fixedly into mine.

In the workshop they closed all the doors and windows and my father took the sheep shears down from the shelf. Old Pyp got busy stirring a tin of white paint with a stick. I felt nauseous and went outside, past the bundle on the workbench.

Behind me I heard the sounds of a tussle, a few exclamations and then the *click-click* of the shears. After a while the monkey began chattering in distress.

I hurried off to the kitchen and asked Mina for a cup of coffee.

The kwedini's laughter drew me out again in spite of myself. With a suffocating feeling in my chest I followed the noise. The monkey was sitting in one of the fowl-runs, sickly naked and white.

'Oh, no ...'

Pa looked serious and he avoided my eyes. Old Pyp stood near the wire netting and mocked the monkey. I felt like putting a bullet in his back.

'When are we going to let him out? When are we going to let him out?' Tattie's eyes were shining. He grabbed Fielies's wire car and took it for a spin round the fowl-run.

'He looks a real freak!' chirped Fielies.

'Like a tokkelosh,' added Figile.

'Come,' my father called me, 'let's have tea first. We'll let him out this afternoon when the other monkeys come down to the river to drink.'

I hesitated. 'Pa ... tell them to leave him alone ...' My father looked at me and then said a few words to the others. They slunk off disappointedly. At the front door, before we went in, I looked back. The white monkey was hanging from the side of the run and gnawing at the wire netting with his small teeth.

Later that afternoon we stood round the fowl-run. Tattie and co. could hardly contain their excitement; Jock had recovered his self-confidence and pressed himself against the run, his tail stiff, his eyes greedy, as if he wanted to get at the monkey.

'Tie up that dog,' my father ordered. Figile dragged the dog away and Old Pyp went into the run, a stick in one hand, his hat in the other.

'Heaa, heaa,' he shouted. I could see he was a little unsure of himself because the monkey simply sat motionless and stared at him. 'Child of the devil!' He brandished his stick, the kwedini giggled nervously and then the monkey shot past Old Pyp, zipped through the gate and loped rapidly across the yard.

'Run, run, tokkelosh!' The kwedini followed as fast as their legs could carry them, scrambling over the fence and haring after the animal.

My father sighed and turned for home.

I had a sick knot in my stomach and didn't respond to Old Pyp's hoarse joke. Far away down the dusty track to the fields I saw the white monkey running with his grey tail curved. Arched in the air, his tail was the only part of his body they hadn't painted. A long way behind, the kwedini followed, waving their arms.

Suddenly everything seemed terrible, and as I walked past Jock, who was almost strangling on his chain from excitement, I kicked him in the ribs.

By milking time, I couldn't bear it any longer. I had to go and see what had happened to the white monkey. I swung my point-two-two over my shoulder, took my hat and set out for the river.

When I got to the first donga, I heard the monkeys. They were disturbed: chattering and arguing and jumping about in the trees. I bent low through a stand of reeds, picked up one of the monkey trails and went down to the riverbed. They were so preoccupied that their guard, who always sat on one side and kept an eye on the world while they drank, didn't even notice me. I saw them a little way ahead in the bushes.

The white monkey was there too, I could sense it.

Then I saw him. He sat some way to this side of them, facing in their direction. As soon as he moved forward, the troop pulled back, chattering and inquisitive, but also afraid. He inched forward along the branch. Suddenly he let go, plopped down on the sandbank and raced towards them.

The troop leader, a muscular male who had been sitting right in front, sizing up the white monkey, shot round, rolled over and then made off with the rest following him.

I floundered after them through the reeds, tripped and lost my hat, but all the time I couldn't get rid of the memory of the white monkey's pathetic eyes. The reeds slashed at my arms and legs but I hurried on.

Eventually the white monkey stopped, and so did the troop but on the opposite side of the stream from where he sat on a sandbank. I crept closer. The troop made themselves comfortable in the thorn trees and sat there swaying and staring at the white monkey. From where I was I could hear him make soft noises; he scratched himself and turned round. Slowly he climbed up a thorn tree and crouched on a branch.

I held my breath, because now it was dead quiet, and the smallest noise from me would send them all flying, the white monkey as well. Just as silently, almost dreamily, the troop suddenly melted into the trees behind them. A few branches swayed and they were gone.

Step by step I edged towards the tree where the white monkey sat. Then, with my gun slung awkwardly over my back, I crawled on all fours so as not to frighten him away.

Under the tree I rose half upright, so that the trunk of the tree was between me and the monkey. I slid a cartridge into the barrel; it made a cold sound in the late afternoon air.

Quickly I stepped round the trunk, and fired at his face as it swung towards me, ridiculously white on his bare shaven neck.

I knew he was dead from the thump on the sandbank below me. I did not turn. I did not look at his crumpled body.

My Cuban

I have a Cuban on a leash. The loop is slung loosely over my left wrist, just the way they taught us at the SADF Dog and Horse School at Voortrekkerhoogte, where the red powdery dust has been trodden flat. The choke-chain round the Cuban's neck does not cause pain if I jerk it, only gives a sharp shock to remind him about the importance of discipline.

Even Barbara Woodhouse explained these basic principles to the nation, with a pastoral English scene in the background. These are things that any corporal in the Dog Division is familiar with.

I have not yet cut off the Cuban's ear. This act of ecstasy, which derives from the Americas (even nearer to the Cuban's motherland than stinking, pillaged Angola), will take place later. Like the Red Indians, I will only exact my trophy at the end, right at the very end. I will salt it carefully, pack it in cotton wool and send it by military airmail to Bellville where the family will preserve it in formalin and display it to admiring guests when they come visiting on Sunday afternoons. Or, at my request, nail it to the front door jamb.

So that they who have ears to hear can hear.

It sounds savage. War is like that. But on the other hand love is also savage.

I don't say this in order to avoid the issue. Having been through a six-week patrol in the bush, only now do I really understand what the newspapers or the weather bureau means by *searing* heat. There is so much meaning contained in that one word: the shrill song of the cicadas that penetrates everything like radio waves, through bone, through flesh, through marrow. Also the sweat that hangs in drops from your eyebrows; if you look up momentarily (as you shouldn't do) you see the drops. The green bush, green fatigues, the blotches of other bodies, the shifting dappled light, the sun that breaks through and the slog with the only body that you have. Searing.

So I am not digressing. I am coming to the unique relationship between me and the Cuban. We were destined to find each other. As in the old slave trade. (They say that Portuguese girls – some bastardised, unfortunately – are for sale just a little further north than the Rooikat Operational Area. We haven't been that far yet but they say the Recces are fucking around up there.) First I looked him over thoroughly. His molars were in good shape. His front teeth had been slightly discoloured by the Havanna cigars he'd smoked. But his nostrils were pleasingly fine-chiselled. His hands were elegant and on the whole I couldn't complain.

What the others got hold of was ... oh well.

I took my Cuban with me everywhere I went. That was the golden rule. Never be without your Cuban, said the commandant.

Because the Total Onslaught demanded Total Preparedness.

My Cuban and I conversed.

Me: What has this Castro got?

Him:

Me: Would you choose to die by mortar, Stalin-organ, AK-47 or bayonet?

He:

Me: The Swapos sometimes tie you down over an anthill. The ants go for the soft moist places first – the mouth and other openings. People are like that too: we eat the cherries on the cake first. And the ants aren't really guilty. They don't know what they are doing. Ultimately, they do not know pain. The writhing, screaming body of the victim is no more than a great edible morsel. They do not recognise the life, the priceless life in it. They cannot place a value on intelligence. The spark of personality goes right over their heads, as do individual characteristics. In short, this is simply a meal for them. They are driven only by a dumb and mindless but profound urge. They have to eat and they march with the relentlessness that comes from generations of inbred instinct. And so I do not blame the ants. Whom do you blame?

He:

Me: Perhaps we should explain to the reader how I came upon you. We don't want the readers to feel, as we do, that they are swaying about in the wind, puppets on strings that make comical jerky movements when there's the movement of a finger. Above all, the reader must not feel like a yo-yo, continuously projected into a space where he feels unstructured and endangered. Instead we will deceive him with the known and see what that achieves.

He:

Me: Come on, sit still now. I am going to tie you up outside tonight in the rain – if it rains – as the others do sometimes; do you think it will rain?

He:

Me: It was quite some time after the Bridge Fourteen episode. Or saga. Or victory. I mention that to orientate the reader. Al Venter had just been here to shoot *Into Angola* for SATV. He'd inevitably focused his cameras selectively here and there. From the shadows I watched the broken children hobbling round him, vying with the fat nurses for a place in front of the lens. And the readers no doubt also saw how the foil-wrapped flesh was later unloaded, as if it were a supermarket.

As savage as love, that is war. As I have already said.

The parachutes drift like downy feathers, each with a little weight hanging from it. They drift like thistledown with the seed underneath. How wonderfully nature planned her systems! The wind bears the seed under its downy parachute to a patch of ground where it can fall, germinate and live.

I was one of these thistle seeds. Oh, how we drifted, the beautiful young men of the Republic. Green were our uniforms, red the flush on our cheeks, the wind rushing by us and Africa like a hand stretched open beneath us – and away, away droned the aircraft and under us, lower down, over the tops of the bush, the helicopters churned with their red crosses. Sweetly we descended in the sun, the wind, my God! I was so close, yet so far. In the blink of an eye everything could change. Death/life, just like that, with the border between the two as incidental and fine as the degree of the variant in the aim of a gun barrel.

Thistle seeds, heroic deeds. Sons of the Republic: Africa is ours, ours the white down feathers.

Lie still, Cuban, no food for you today. Listen to the tin plates clattering in the sink. A crippled former Swapo soldier does the washing up. He stands on one leg and watches with one eye as the shiny plates slide off into the greasy washing-up water. He stands under a tarpaulin cover under the only tree and watches how the left-overs are scraped into a drum until it's piled high and bored boots tread it down and later the men lie twitching like young dogs, bare chested in the tents, turning photos of their loved ones round and round in their hands or carrying them off to the latrines.

Love is savage, sometimes just as savage as war.

It was shortly after the last visit of Al Venter and SATV. Operation Kudu was still in the planning stage. We didn't know, but we had heard anyway. That's the way it goes among the tents (it was always like an ants' nest), the whispers grow to rumours and the rumours to news and the news is promulgated as fact and general knowledge. It wasn't so yet but it was so: we would go in deeper than ever before, deep, deep into the ravaged land, past the ruins and abandoned tractors and cars and delivery vans, past the ruins of Portuguese shops and past clusters of wanderers who waited with wide hysterical eyes for the Jeeps and Bedfords to come and go. We would break through, through Savimbi's territory over the savannah almost as far as – or, yes, perhaps right into – Luanda.

One great unit would be formed from all the units: a single machine. The idea of penetration roused great excitement, as you can appreciate.

Or like with Jamesy – hey, Cuban, listen – like with Jamesy: they wrapped him up in a fresh cowhide and the women sewed him into the damp cylinder. The gang was off long before the hide dried there under the tree, and we found Jamesy with his tongue hanging onto his chest and seething with a mass of bluebottle flies. We buried him like that, just like that, inside his coffin of dried cowhide.

How long does it take a cowhide to dry and shrink in the Angolan sun?

Jamesy was half Dutch, the cheese-head of the camp. He still had one foot in the Netherlands. On patrol he took off Gerrit Achterberg or Nijhoff and I found it hysterically funny – the cosmic revolt and "Voor dag en dauw" in the Angolan bush. We were over the border – his Netherlands a mild little land somewhere out of our collective unconscious. And so Jamesy Zeeman, previously from Amsterdam, died of cowhide shrinkage.

What happened to the conversation between me and my Cuban? He never answered, and if he had wanted to ... well, I don't understand his language. I wonder what language he speaks? Has Cuba got its own language? They never told us. The cigars were good. They lay amongst the corpses in underground bunkers or smouldered in dead fingers. The smoke was still in the warm lungs as we dragged them out of the bunkers; and when we tossed them like mattresses onto the Bedfords, they fell with a thud and the dead lungs coughed out blue smoke.

Their souls had already been back in Cuba for ages, I reckoned.

In any case, we had been instructed not to converse more than necessary with the Cubans. They had also no doubt received the classic command: name, rank and number. Nothing more. Even if they treat you like a dog. Or spread-eagle you over an anthill.

Operation Kudu was still on the drawing-board, forming itself in the brilliant minds of the strategists: a Disneyland of power and shrapnel and violence and bucking Jeeps and rattling firearms and flesh that suddenly burst through skin and the frightening white splinter of bone. I am not just saying this. I was there.

Others were not there. Some of the guys – and not all of them were Nusas members either, please note – who had been at Bridge Fourteen and beyond went awol. Never again, they said. The territory was too foreign. They hailed (for example) from cosmopolitan Sea Point. They had always lived there. Now they'd landed in Angola. They – oh well, I can sympathise. It was like with Jamesy Zeeman: somewhere there is a short circuit.

A lot of guys went awol. In one camp it was apparently over lousy food. We knew that it was actually over Operation Kudu. But the big shots didn't know that we knew. Everyone knew that we knew, from rifleman up to the rank of first lieutenant. Higher up they believed it was only they that knew: those who carried batons under their arm and strutted about like peacocks in the mess at night.

We knew, and prepared ourselves. How does a soldier

prepare himself? He bids farewell to things that he cannot be parted from. He's not like a chap on Death Row. He doesn't know. What you actually say goodbye to is certainty. You say goodbye to certainty and that takes quite a while. It takes a good many nights. It takes a lot of thinking, or a lot of thinking away. Some guys think it away. They go mad: the camp is a crazy place before an operation. They drink and fight like pit bulls. They swear and bugger up the latrines. They steal Bedfords and dice through the refugee camp. They tie the gays naked onto the bonnets of Jeeps and race to town with them. They drink, drink, drink.

Of the other chaps who just think, some leave. They go awol. They can't go home because that's the first place they'll be looked for. They go awol to the YMCA in Durban, Port Elizabeth, Cape Town or Johannesburg ... but eventually they can't even go there. The big shots have a permanent watch on the YMCAs to keep an eye on them. Could one say that it was a whole generation gone awol? What do you think, Cuban?

He:

Me: Away from a war they didn't understand? And you, you are also from an island and you also fight somewhere else – another continent. Or is your fatherland just an idea?

He:

Me: Operation Kudu was announced on the daily orders. The officers wanted to prepare us; on the big day they gently broke the news that we were going in. But we already knew. We were already prepared.

That was quite a while back. Since then I got my Cuban and he is the result of everything that happened in the meantime.

My whole life has changed since I got this Cuban. I cannot leave him alone. He is always with me. A part of me, you might say. We are, as the saying goes, one. If I go down to the latrine block, he has to come too. If I go to shower, he must also share those private moments. He is so close to me that he shares my dreams. He almost knows what I think.

Me: Hey, Cuban, do you agree? Is it so?

He doesn't answer, doesn't look at me, like a cowed dog too afraid to look at its master. I jingle the choke-chain. It sounds like something in a medieval dungeon or in a Barbara Woodhouse programme.

We had a premonition of it. Each one had the premonition – after Operation Kudu, his life would never be the same again. Some of the guys reached this conclusion melodramatically. Others thought it out quietly. I believe that I felt it instinctively, on a more realistic plane than the others.

In comparison, the small patrols into the bush (which I have already referred to) began to seem like Boy Scout expeditions to the Vaal Dam or Chapman's Peak. Something bigger lay ahead, my Cuban, something that bestowed you on me, that brought you to me, so that now I have you with me just as one carries a fragment of shrapnel in one's thigh – you are never without the nagging pain, never free of the memory.

Thistle seeds. Heroic deeds. Inside the aircraft the drone of the engines deadened everything. It always made me think of insects: the huge helmets with the net fastened onto them. The rucksacks with the stubby guns, waterbottles on hips, daubed faces. Like insects in the belly of a greater insect. In times like these, people also sought out the soft damp places first. There are things you think about, things that haunt you. And this is when love becomes more savage than war. Ultimately you lose all sense of fear. The plains that slide by beneath you are simply a chart, the chart that was drilled into you at Base, before departure. You are a pin; if you move with tactical precision, the blue pin on the chart becomes a little flag. If you or one of the others in your squad makes a mistake, the pin is removed and all that remains on the chart is a small hole.

You have forgotten you are life, priceless life. You are therefore no longer afraid to die. This is the secret of all armies. This is the magical power of the uniform, the tribal dance, the marching squad, the aircraft in formation.

Thistle seeds, hero's deeds. Inside the aircraft: the smell of Africa's wind is not Etosha's mud or the heavy fragrance of the tropics, it is not the smell of fresh dung and grass and the early morning. Africa's smell is a mixture of engine oil, sweat, leather, boot polish, garments, canvas, rubber, semen, flesh, blood and the sharp reek given off by a body in the highest state of anxiety – anxiety not as fear but as hyper-preparedness, adrenalin-anxiety. It is the breath, the new breath of the continent.

We knew it was time to get ready. The engines were throttled back, the red light flashed on. Quickly, too quickly, the time had come. The cabin door gaped, a chasm to a dark and savage land below. The smell grew suffocating. The smell of Africa. We sweated, the sweat and camouflage paint was smudged off onto the backs of hands. You wanted to jump, to get out into the sweet breezes, into the free fall where there was no turning back. You wanted just to fall and fall, an independent bullet, a missile aimed at the centre of the earth.

I have to jump. The air tugs at my cheeks. My mind is blank. Concentrate only on the jump, the mechanics drilled into me at parachute school. I fall free of the aircraft, the great steel bird that is quickly gone; I can see its shadow slipping over the bush below and to the left. Below me the white blooms of a couple of open 'chutes, ruins, a rusted iron roof still reflecting the sun. I tug my canopy and pull into a peaceful sweep. I am now in the no-man's-land where all certainty is gone. No earth beneath my feet, no propeller to bear me away, no knowledge of what awaits me below. Like thistledown, delivered to the mercy of the wind and chance and – according to the chaplain – Providence, I drifted.

I was to be completely alone until we formed up again on the ground after unclipping from our canopies. I had to control my fear. Think of the operation. Think of every movement. Check over my gun mentally. Try to steer my canopy. Look out for an enemy patrol. The foreign land came closer and closer. I fell like a seed – with a death or a life within.

I did not expect the Cuban. I didn't ask for him. He was forced upon me – by the times, by history, the particular political circumstances. But how ever he, for his part, landed up there (by chance or Providence) – the fact is, when I touched down in a whirlwind, half skew in a bush which stood about man-high, with my canopy billowing out to one side in the wind and I braking and floundering and swearing and looking around me for the other guys – then the Cuban was there.

Sallow as an islander, foreign, with the chiselled nostrils and the sensual nostrils, he stepped out of the shadow and into a splash of sunlight, his cream-coloured uniform brand new, an immaculate fit on his body. Did he smile at me? Swearing, I tried to disentangle myself from my harness, the winged anchor that bound me. At last I was free, the short carbine in my hands, warm with the sun that had already penetrated the metal still half in the bush I fell and the carbine started to chatter beneath me and the dust rose in small vertical spurts around the Cuban's boots but yet he still came on smiling and I cursed him and his line and his whore of a mother and his island and still smiling he kept coming but he never got to me where I lay and shot my carbine empty, sobbing, still half in my harness, with the parachute languidly rising and falling in the breath of Africa.

My Afrikaner

You aren't a real Boer, are you? No broad-brimmed hat, bandoleer and guerilla attacks on the imported pink soldiers of a fat queen. No Victoria for you, Boer without a bandoleer. You sit there in your cage with the green pack of ten-rand notes in your fingers. While we give your mates the water treatment in the hut, I see how you count the notes over and over again. He can keep the leaves, the comrade commander had said, because he is a moneylender for a lost republic. Play on with your notes, my boer, just as your forefathers sat and played on St Helena. You are no more. You burnt your own bridges. For I see the love of pain in your eyes, when you gaze through the wire netting at me where I sit under the tree with my gun on my knees.

You have loved me, my boer, from the first moment when I dragged you by one leg from the hollow anthill and you didn't scream like a stuck pig (as the media commissar and I had hoped you would) but lay silent on your stomach. What did you mutter, white corporal, soldier from the south, here so far from your ancestors and your regime?

Yes, I am not a pink Khaki from another land. I am black, my boer, black as Africa. You will not recognise me, my face is unknown to you. But you reminded me of faces from my boyhood. White faces. Yes, I pretend I cannot understand your language. I make as if your words are foreign to me, there where you sit on the ground in your pen holding a note up to the sun and looking at the shadowy springbok head concealed in the fabric of the note.

You were sawing your wrists open with the springbok head off your beret when we captured you. There was blood, my comrade boer, my Afrikaner, springbok blood in your black Mass of self-destruction. You knew what awaited you if we caught you: an island. In a hut in a bush that you did not know, without north or south, without a single word of affection. With the onslaught that I launch, three times a day, on your body. You become my dog, your body my hunting ground: your loins, your throat, your penis that shrinks back when you see me coming; I can see your balls withdraw into your body from fear, I see how the veins on your underarms contract and disappear.

You fear me, don't you? One day we will indeed meet, me and your greedy tongue, when you can no longer rein back your words, when you have been tried beyond endurance, my brave Afrikaner, when the caress of my hot irons on your skin gets to be too much.

You didn't just come out of any old anthill, my Afrikaner. No, from your hands I could tell that you had done gentlemanly work in a city. You worked with paper, and when I see how you arrange the notes around you in a circle and sit in the middle of it, I imagine that you worked with money and that you barricaded yourself with money just as your forefathers drew their wagons up in a circle around them. Against my forefathers. Against the onslaught of pain.

I, my Afrikaner, was educated in pain. My university was different from yours. My degree in pain is higher than yours. That's how they educated us in that bush college. Do you know how much trouble they went to with us, those professors with pistols on their hips and scars on their faces? Civilised pain does not exist, they told us. You are qualified in pain, they said.

That is why I reach out to you so tenderly when it is our turn in the hut. Just you and I. Did you realise a black man could be so tender? No, you didn't realise. You thought a black man was only good for throwing stones, or manning the petrol pump while you waited impatiently with your glossy car and the ten-rand note in your hand, or fornicating like a rat in his black shanty among all the other shanties.

I feel sorry for you, comrade, because here you must learn to know. Here is no neat suburban street down which you can disappear, behind your mailbox and your burglar alarm and your anti-theft devices and your policies and your money.

Here am I, now.

And here are you, now.

It is as if my whole system had waited for this: you know, like a man sometimes waits when he's hunting. He can see the buck moving in the undergrowth, he can see the markings of its hide, but beyond that it is just a blur in the vision. He can take a chance and shoot, but it would most likely only wound the animal. And, my Afrikaner, wounding is something we don't want to do. No, we'd rather wait until the buck's slender ears show above the shrubs, then a delicate ankle, then a hip, then his slim neck and then, at last, the shoulder, fat and glossy and ripe for death. The bullet, my Afrikaner, we save for the very last, once we have seen your whole body. The sleekness and the suppleness of it, the sinews moving under the skin, the joints that swivel in their sockets and suddenly crack in my hand when I press so gently and carefully and you cringe away from me with staring eyes.

First I want to get to know you and see how yours differ from mine. How your fingers crack differently from mine, how the arch of your instep is higher, or the cartilage of your ear folds more easily. But in the mornings, squatting and groaning in the corner of your pen, you do just as I do. And at dawn when you hug your arms around yourself, you have gooseflesh just as I do. And at night when you cry, alone in your cage after our midday session in the hut, then you sound just like the women in the townships.

You are not different, my Afrikaner, and that's to your disadvantage because we now have no excuse to spin death out much longer. There is nothing strange that we can study. There is nothing. You are naked and you are nothing, as I am. Do you hear me? There where you arrange your banknotes in patterns. They are all we allowed you to keep – now you cannot even buy eternal rest with them.

Perhaps you could chew them into wet pellets and stuff them into your ears while we give your mates the water treatment in the hut. The Khakis, according to your history books, were afraid of the hot sun of Africa. The Afrikaners, it seems to me, my comrade, are afraid of the water of Africa.

You must listen to them. I know you listen. So that, when you and I go in, you know that there were others, from other cages, so that you know that we are not going to walk along this path alone. You can smell it too when we enter the hut, the hut that the comrade commissar equipped for our interrogations. You smell fear and you block your nose. You smell sweat and I see how your temples get wet the minute you smell the sweat of your mates. You see the wet patterns made by their bodies on the tarpaulin, you see how elbows can dig holes in the ground, you see how heels can drum loose the surface of the cowdung floor and you know, my Afrikaner: it is now you and I.

I don't ask questions because I know you are too brave. You would not answer the kind of questions that the commissar orders. And I don't ask my own questions, because I know that you know what the answers are that I seek. We are past questions and answers, I believe. And while I use my hands and the techniques I learned in that bush college in the far north (I was the best student), there is only the writhing of your body and the no-man's-land between my unasked questions and your unspoken answers.

Once, while I was slipping the waterpipe carefully down your throat, you asked me in Afrikaans if I would help you to escape. I don't understand your words, my comrade, had you forgotten? I know the language, yes, and I hear how sweetly it sits on your broken tongue. It opens up memories for me, places and people and names. But, all the same, you know: I do not understand it.

And even if you try to break me open with the words of places that I know, I will not give in. I can see that you see when a word touches my heart. If it touches a place or a person that I have stored away deeply. But I will not give in. I will maintain silence. Just like you. You will not find comprehension in me. When you ask me, Do you have a wife?, I do not hear. Wife is not a word that I want to know. She sits far away in a hut in a homeland or an administration house. I do not know where the administration trucks have carted her. I do not know how long the officials allowed her to live in one place. I took off during the first rain of stones, in the year of the children, when we pulled the adults back and went out in front, into the bullets and the cells and the bush. Over the borders. Without knowing what lay ahead. Stupid, maybe, because we expected a short struggle. Something better.

You won't break me open, not with your words, my Afrikaner, because I am a man with no land. My feet seek only the paths in the bush, the hell camps in the bush in Angola and Mozambique; my mouth has learned to get hold of words that are foreign to you. My language is the language of a thing unknown to you.

And although I try to explain this to you with my fire-irons, my pipes and my hooks, although I fish about in your orifices, although I fasten your tongue with a wire, although I delve about in your softest parts, you still ask me: have you a wife?

I do not understand love. You try to trap me with the one love that you think I know, my beloved Afrikaner, but you know nothing of the loves that keep me on these footpaths, in these bunkers, in these huts of martyrdom.

You must finish your game with the ten-rand notes, it's nearly time for our turn. I can hardly wait because I find the barbed-wire between us tedious: me in the shade with your R-1 on my knee and only the smell of gun oil and the tinned fish which I didn't finish eating and put down beside me, and you in your cage, with your naked body trying to squeeze itself into the narrow shadow of the fencepost and your eyes fixed on your banknotes.

How do you like your new fatherland, comrade Afrikaner? the commander asked when he came past you here and you, my drunk Afrikaner (I smuggle it in for you, they don't know that), held a note out to him. There's nothing to buy here, the commandant told you. But you must not judge him too hastily, my Afrikaner. He is a man who knows pain better than you and I. His father is sitting on your prison island, his mother is on her knees with a scrubbing brush in the shining passage of a dominee's house, for two rand a day, he tells me, my comrade, and he himself spent a long time in your cells.

And he is filled with hate, my Afrikaner. He is not like you and me. He would not put the instruments down if he saw you could not take any more, if he saw you were no longer in your eyes. When the thing you didn't know existed comes to sit in your eyes. He would not realise, like I do, that your silences are filled with answers. That my questions have dwelt within you for a long time and your answers in me. He is a man of war.

You must prepare yourself because the day will come when he takes you over from me. He will just walk in here with his quirt and pistol and say: Give him to me. Then it is no longer just pain, my Afrikaner. Then pain is nothing.

He will show you other things that you did not know existed. You will get drunk from nausea, you will get intoxicated from your own puke, you will fall unconscious because your brain will not believe it. And maybe it will kill you. Perhaps it will rob you of your answers.

I know the bush is not for you. Never ask me again – as you did the day before yesterday – which way is south. Look in any direction and hope it is south. South no longer exists – it is just a direction of the wind. And your money no longer exists, because it can't buy anything. And your words no longer exist because we do not understand.

I can repeat your words to you, because I know them. They are the same words churning in my mind. Two days ago, when you asked me which way was south, I sat here and counted them. Pretty words, Afrikaans words. About sixty, I make it. And they tumble in your thoughts and jerk in your throat and stick fast on your tongue when I link the electrodes to you. I know them so well: perhaps, when the comrade commander takes you over from me, I will whisper them to you, quietly, in your language. Because they are mine too. I carry them with me along the footpaths and when I stalk through the bush. I had them in me when I dragged you out of the anthill and you refused to bleat like a goat and I kicked you in the face for the comrade commissar. Then they rose, unbidden, in me. Words that would make a man of the bush ashamed, my comrade. That is why I store them away, before I hand you over to the comrade commander. He and the political commissar have their own words – those words are their fatherland, until they have driven the Afrikaner from his cage.

At the university overseas they said I was the cleverest

they'd ever had from a township. In Soweto I had to write the pamphlets for the children who danced before the Casspirs. Ha, and couldn't I write them well! I didn't even need to think, my comrade, the words came rushing out, the wonderful slogans of hate, and I may tell you, as you creep up close to the wire netting and carefully listen to me with your bloodied ear, that I also wrote them in the forbidden language that was used to accuse and curse and ban and remove my people.

But now it is the language of silence, my comrade, like your sixty words of love and longing, of freedom and peace, of faith and dreams.

Freedom for me is not freedom for you. Longing for me is not longing for you. They have two faces, all these words of yours. Nothing is the same, my Afrikaner, not even faith. That is why I ask in silence and you answer in silence.

It was a long long journey for me from that narrow street with no street lights in Soweto, the city where the smoke swirls when the sun sets, the city of yellow winter grass, coal fires, burning cars on street corners. I was over the border on the back of a bouncing truck.

I could not speak the language of politics. I wanted freedom, freedom! First I had to sit and listen, for hours on end with headphones over my ears and closed eyes. I had to forget your language, my Afrikaner, and learn the new language, other words that formed clumsily on my tongue, and I had to speak them without fear or prompting. Then there were the tests, and finally the foreign harbour with people diving after the coins thrown from ships by the tourists. After the ship with cannons draped in fishnet there was the big university and foreign people where I sang the songs of my childhood softly to myself and thought of my mother's coal fire.

I was far away and I realised that I loved my fatherland. Would you believe that, my Afrikaner? A black man who loves the land you fought Queen Victoria for? For which your women died in the concentration camp?

Why, do you imagine, my Afrikaner, does the political commissar come to have a look at you every day? Because without you he will never be free. He is not checking that I give you enough scars and you bleed enough. He comes to your cage, with your turds in the corner, the drag marks you leave when you crawl across the floor, the ten-rand notes that are getting grubbier and bloodier. He sees his freedom.

In my love, my Afrikaner, I see my hate. I will caress the places that hurt and ask you nothing, because I am afraid you will say something that spoils it. I am afraid you'll give in. I am afraid, my Afrikaner, that you'll abandon your courageous suffering.

We are about the same age, we probably weigh the same although I have picked up a bit of weight through sitting around in the camp and you are losing weight. Our feet are about the same size, and judging by your shoulders, we are probably evenly matched in strength. And I often think: when I was born in a hut with a candle and I lay on some old rags beside my bleeding mother and a goat bleated outside (it was in a 'reserve' as you called it), you most likely slid out into the soft white cloth held by a clever doctor to catch you, and then straight into an incubator. And when you learnt to write in a clean white exercise book, covered by your mother in brown paper and plastic, I and three others tried to scratch on a slate all at the same time with grubby fingers.

And for this reason, my Afrikaner, we speak two different languages.

When the aircraft comes over and you all tumble out and drift down under your parachutes, then I wonder.

You must not think, my Afrikaner, that I am not completely committed to the struggle. I'll take a bullet if I have to. In spite of the sixty words. And you, my Afrikaner, will also take it like a man – I can see that. But now you must learn what it feels like to live five paces from your own excrement, week after week. You must smell the smell of your own pain, all the smells your body gives off when it thinks it can go no further.

Learn, learn my Afrikaner, learn, learn, I say in my thoughts as I stroke the instruments over your flanks. Feel how your flesh answers. The flesh is not yet dead. The flesh lives in pain. And don't grab me like that. Grab yourself, rather. Turn your back to me and the other guards and take hold of yourself. Learn that there is still a pleasant thrill locked up in your body. That the body can still give pleasure.

Oh, how we danced! The young youths, the youngest of the young! In front of the Casspirs with our wonderful songs! Flames flickering behind our dances, teargas drifting among us on the winds of that frightful winter. It was a physical thrill, it was pain, it was joy. Freedom lay ahead, the new day beckoned. And we were the youngest of the young, the foremost, the brave ones.

We were free. We buried the dead as though they lived! We jubilantly sang out our message for the cameras. We christened traitors with petrol and set them alight. We challenged each other to make our bodies thinner before the bullets.

That was before the hell camps, the comrades with their pistols, the other universities.

And when we were called, we listened to the merchants of ideology and, my Afrikaner, we are still trying to return. This time more filled with rage because we are not sure what we have lost. This time stronger because we hope for victory. This time poorer, and perhaps more disillusioned, but this time with so little to lose that the commander and the political commissar have to come and stand at your cage every day to stoke the fires of bitterness, to refresh their anger, to deny the sixty words, to inflict pain and feed on pain like bread.

It is a struggle, my Afrikaner, that has slipped through your fingers and which you do not understand, because already the commander and the political commissar are eyeing each other at night from their sleeping places, when the monkeys chatter in the high trees and the moon hangs scarlet on the horizon. They are already counting heads, the deeper we withdraw into the bush. After every skirmish they imagine that one of their own people was also firing on them. One of these days, my Afrikaner, they will forget you and take up the irons against each other. Have you already thought of that as your only hope?

My Afrikaner, when I stand guard in the long grass of the plain and listen to the tribespeople singing and I hear the commissar's and the commander's voices rise and fall as they bend over the chart in the light of the oil lamp, then I think of the thousands of others like you and me. I think about the sixty words that they carry around with them, and I think not one of them is as brave as you are, not one of them loves the pain as much as you and I in this merciless bush.

Ha, it's a long way, my Afrikaner, to go and fetch your freedom. And the road back is even more difficult. But we have learnt enough words. Johannesburg and Durban are in flames, and in Uitenhage the police are already interrogating themselves. It is a long way to go and fetch freedom.

Why do you never curse me? I know all your groans, I know the boundaries of your pain so well. The hut smells of straw and cowdung. It is so airless in there. It makes me think of slaughtering a goat, when one cuts the belly open and draws the muscle aside and the entrails tumble out, warm and steaming. That is how it smells when you and I are at work in there, my Afrikaner. But why do you never curse me? Why are you so stingy with your Afrikaans words? Burn him, the commissar told me, until he calls you a kaffir and then we will take him over.

But, my Afrikaner, you are so stingy here in your cage. And you are even stingier in the hut.

The only thing you are still generous with are those ten-rand notes that you hold out to the commander every day when he comes to stand at your cage.

If someone comes forward one day and asks, Why?, I will tell him that the bush does not recognise reasons, my Afrikaner. Even though we are equally broad of shoulder, our weight almost the same, even though we share sixty words.

Afrikaner, be true to me. Do not ask me again to thrust the iron deeper to where your life ends and your death begins. Stay with me as long as the war lasts.

As long as my Soweto and my Uitenhage burn, stay with me.

But come on now, the time is at hand. For you to find your dreams in pain once again. Perhaps in our dreams we find one another, in a quiet country where we can say everything that is to be said.

Come, my beloved Afrikaner, the fire-irons await us.

Trains

Stationmaster Ferreira came out of the toilet shed where he'd been sitting, contemplating, while a narrow ray of sunlight pierced through a small hole in the corrugated-iron door and shafted past his head. From where he sat, if he tilted his head a fraction, that ray shot him full in the face, it was as if it woke him from the heat, and then he'd think again, behind the corrugated-iron door, among the buzzing blue-bottle flies, about the station, the railway lines on either side, and about his wife and child.

Now he pulled the door closed behind him, fumbling with his fly, screwing up his eyes against the merciless sunlight.

Behind the railway halt lay a straggling mountain range, parallel with the gleaming railway lines that shot off on either side of the station building. This is the hard Karoo, the sprawling mountains are brown and rough, and sometimes at dusk they resemble one of those enormous animals that lumbered through swamps in this world centuries ago.

The only green that met his eyes was a clump of pepper trees with little banks of earth round their roots. Between trains, like now, he came out of the building and carried a can of water to each tree. The water came sprinkling brightly from the nozzle and was almost immediately sucked up by the earth.

There was something wrong with his wife, he thought, while he shook the last drops from the nozzle. In the evening when he was off duty and walked up the gravel path to the front door, the child would be playing in the dust near the garden path. The child had a couple of little cars that he pushed around in the dust incessantly. When he heard the gate and looked up and saw his father, interest flickered briefly in his eyes.

But then he went back to playing, grading dust roads with his hand or sitting at the empty fish pond staring at the rusty tins and shards of glass which lay at the bottom.

That was the child. A little bit retarded in intelligence, the school had written, putting the child back into the class where they worked with their hands, weaving baskets and hoeing in the garden.

That was when his wife had gone quiet. Or was it only then that he noticed it? She'd always complained about the loneliness – the spaces here were wide and empty – when he walked away to the station in the morning and the school bus stopped in front of the house to pick up the child. And the struggle with the garden. The only things that would grow were geraniums and succulents, and if there was a drought, even they died.

And she had started to drink. In the evenings when he came home, there was at first only a slight sourness on her breath. It got worse. One evening the child was not beside the garden path. The house was empty although the doors and windows were open. He picked up their tracks; she had walked into the veld with the child. He found them in a dry stream bed. She was sitting with her back against the one bank crying while the child pulled her arm saying, 'Oh, come on, Ma, come on Ma…'

This was the middle of nowhere, she had said. Only the trains came by, full of shiny cars from General Motors in transit inland from Port Elizabeth. Red ones and yellow ones and green ones, and even the child stood open-mouthed as the trucks with the strings of new cars rushed by.

'Where are all the cars going to?' his wife always asked. But he knew she didn't really want an answer. She wanted to say, 'Let's go to the city too, or to a town ...' There are flies here and by eleven o'clock the house is full of dust again, even if you've cleaned it out at nine; the dust creeps over the threshold, filters through the gauze screen right into the carpets and blankets and mattresses.

And the passenger trains came by, at night, with their compartments lit up and the people going somewhere, just anywhere away from here, she always whined.

Just anywhere away from here.

At half past five, stationmaster Ferreira handed over to the man on night duty, who travelled the twenty kilometres from town. He walked home with his tin box. The sun was already setting and he thought of how many trains had passed through his signals that day.

He walked past the child near the garden path. The child was humming over his cars. Once he'd bought a small locomotive for the child. It had been lost and later he had found it lying in the fowl run.

The screen slammed closed behind him, and a small cloud of flies buzzed around his ears before settling on the gauze again.

He called his wife. She didn't answer. He went to the bedroom. She sat on the bed and watched as he put his briefcase down, took off his black jacket and hung his cap behind the door.

'Good evening,' he said.

She didn't answer but continued to look at him.

'The food is on the table,' she said at last. He went to the kitchen and sat down. He rolled up the sleeves of his black shirt. He called the child, who slammed the gauze screen unnecessarily hard.

'Pa has told you before you must close the door gently.' The child said nothing. Perhaps he'd answered, but a train was rumbling by.

At first, when they hadn't been here long, the trains had woken them up at night because the lines passed close to the house. But eventually the noise of the trains became just another kind of silence. You heard them, but at the same time you didn't hear them. He buttered his bread and cut pieces of melon. He poured coffee for himself and the child, who stared at him silently across the table.

'How's it going at school?' he asked.

'I made a tea tray,' the child said through a mouthful of food.

Outside dusk fell and it seemed to grow warmer. He stood up and lit the oil lamp. The evening was coming, the night. And sometimes he lay beside his wife and wished the morning would come so that he could go to his shiny station and throw the levers that made the signals rise or fall.

She didn't understand.

Suddenly she appeared in the doorway. How creased her frock was, and the shadows cast by the lamplight made her appear old.

'We must leave,' she said.

He chewed without answering.

She didn't understand. She stood in the doorway and stared at him.

'The child's report has come,' she said. 'He has failed.'

He looked at the child. The child looked through the screen door and out into the night.

'I made a tea tray,' the child said. Suddenly he jumped up, shoved the screen door open and ran outside.

'We must go away,' said the woman.

'No,' he said. 'No.'

'The child must go to a special school,' she whined.

'Then we'll send him.'

Suddenly she sat down on the child's chair and looked

at him across the table. 'Then I would be alone in this … shack …' Her mouth was drawn in a bitter line.

He shrugged. 'Only a few years, Martha, then I'll be transferred to a bigger station, then …' And she started to cry, as usual. He wanted to tell her about his signal room; the signals that waited upright beside the track until he threw the levers. And as he threw them, that minute, that second, the great diesels began to roar, and the mighty bodies shuddered into life. But first they had to wait with their trucks filled with uranium or holiday-makers, wait, wait, wait – until he threw the levers.

Then the train roared past the platform, smelling of diesel and oil, the silence split open and a wind rustled through the pepper trees, and then, suddenly, it was silent again.

The train had disappeared into the water.

But she went to the bedroom and he sat silent.

She didn't understand. It was his station, *his*. And there were too many stationmasters in a big town. Too many trains and sidings, it was different from here.

He heard her crying behind the closed door. And the child fiddled about outside in the darkness.

He cut another slice of bread and another train passed, with a noise that filled the whole house and smothered the woman's weeping and made the child stand still outside in the darkness and listen wide-eyed.

When he went to work the next day, down near the shining tracks, the sun was already blazing down on his neck. It was only just eight o'clock, but the cicadas were already shrilling in the bushes beside the track.

Alongside the station building, encircled by neatly arranged stones, was a lawn. In one corner of this little patch, where the shadow of the station building never fell, no matter what the position of the sun there was a dry spot where the bare earth had already got the upper hand.

Every morning when stationmaster Ferreira walked the two hundred metres from his house to the station building, the shining tracks held his gaze. It was as though the tracks and the sun that struck them led his eyes on and on to the point where the two lines met, in the distance, in one shining blotch on the plains. And if the sun was fierce, as it was today, that blotch hovered a few centimetres above the horizon as though it were liquid.

Then it seemed as though the great puttering diesels dragged their trucks into the water, away from the lawn, the pepper trees and the line of red fire-buckets next to the signal room.

The red buckets were filled with sand.

And every morning, case in hand and sweat already beading on his forehead, he examined the spot of bare ground on the corner of the lawn. If the spot seemed bigger, he took the watering can and that day the pepper trees were neglected. And he removed the cigarette butts that the man on night duty and the conductors threw in the fire buckets when they stood on the platform and smoked of an evening.

It was in the time between the trains that he sat and thought. He sat on the bench in front of the station so that he could see the tracks on both sides. Then he thought about what he could do for Martha.

In the afternoon, at half past three, the stationmaster went to the toilet behind the station building. He'd lowered the signal for the three-forty, because it had to wait for the passenger train from De Aar, which was a non-stop to Port Elizabeth.

And so he had a good twenty minutes to sit in the toilet house and think about Martha and the child, and how it would be at a big station.

The ray of sunshine played on his head, he sat with his head lowered, brushing the flies away continually.

He could already hear the three-forty approaching. The vibrations of the train made the corrugated-iron walls tremble. Suddenly he realised: the train was going by!

He leapt up, buttoning his trousers as he ran, forgetting his cap that hung swaying gently on the hook behind the toilet door. In the signal room he saw immediately what had happened: someone had messed about with the signal levers. He looked out: the signal indicated that the three-forty could proceed past. He ran out onto the platform; the rear end of the conductor's car was already disappearing in the distance. The conductor leaned out and waved to him. He wanted to wave with his cap, realised he didn't have it, so waved his arms, yelling. But the sun and the heat and the roaring of the diesel engines swallowed his voice.

He had to phone. Rushing inside, he had the next stop's number already in mind.

A handkerchief lay on the shiny polished floor in front of the signals. He stopped in his tracks. He remembered the child in the stream bed, tugging at his mother's arm and whining, 'Oh, come on, Ma, come on now, Ma.'

He picked up the handkerchief. It was small, a woman's. The smell was Martha's. Sweet and sultry.

And he stood with his hands on the levers and a numbness crept over him.

Slowly he went to the phone and turned the handle. The next station would stop the passenger train; fortunately it had not yet reached there.

'Is there a problem at Kreerivier?' the stationmaster asked Ferreira.

'No,' he said. 'No. Just stop the passenger train.'

He remembered what she had said when they'd heard about a calf which had been flattened by a train a month earlier.

Ferreira sat on the bench in front of the station. At first

he wanted to phone home, but he knew the child never answered the phone. On each side the tracks stretched out to where the water swallowed them up.

Later he heard something, and from a distance, from the direction of the house, a figure approached. The child. The child walked slowly, preoccupied, as if his thoughts were miles away.

Ferreira stood up to wait for the child. Head down, the child came to stand in front of him; then, looking up, he said, 'I made a tray, Pa.'

Fences

The ritual was the same for my every visit to Zuurpoort. Ceremoniously, Uncle Isaac drew out the brass-bound family Bible and opened it at the front, where our genealogy was recorded.

He began to read in a preachy voice: 'Pieter Wilhelm, eight generations back from you. He farmed on the farm Weltevreden in Tulbagh. His father died in the Netherlands. Pieter Wilhelm is the head of the line.'

His index finger, roughened from farming, moved over the names.

'His son Willem, seven generations removed from you, farmed on De Rietfontein near Ceres. Six generations back from you, your ancestor Jacobus Stephanus married Sophia Emerentia van der Merwe. She was one of the stern Van der Merwes from the Camdeboo. Patriarch Jacobus was the first to farm Zuurpoort.' Uncle Isaac's finger trembled slightly over the curly script. 'Look at the flowery handwriting.' He rested the heavy Bible on his knee.

'Patriarch Jacobus piled up a stone cairn at the head of the valley; an hour's ride on horseback to the north, he made another beacon. Then he rode an hour to the east, made another beacon, an hour to the south and an hour to the west. And so he marked out Zuurpoort.'

From as far back as I can remember Uncle Isaac has been telling this story. And every time it gains fresh meaning: a confirmation of bloodline, the assurance of clan.

'His firstborn, Isaac Petrus, took Zuurpoort over, five generations back. He married a Miss Auret and bought two neighbouring farms, Voetpad and Toorberg. And that's how Zuurpoort came to be the size it is today, two hundred morgen of arable land, eight thousand morgen of hill grazing. Then your great-grandfather, Johann Christoffel Roché took over, married to yet another Van der Merwe from the Camdeboo. After him, your grandfather, also Johann Christoffel Roché, took Zuurpoort over. He married Sophia Emerentia Olivier. My mother.'

The finger moved to the next line: his own name. Isaac Petrus. But as has always been the way before, he did not read his own name. The finger slid down to Boet's name, entered in Uncle Isaac's handwriting.

He sighed. Again, I wanted to ask: Why did Boet join the Permanent Force? Why did he give up everything he was born, bred and brought up for?

Uncle Isaac closed the Bible and fastened the brass clasps. The generator that had throbbed steadily in the background puttered to a halt.

There is nothing quite like the silence that engulfs a farmstead when the generator is switched off at night. Uncle Isaac went to stand before his father's portrait. He sighed again. 'Goodnight, Jac.' The dimly lit house swallowed his footsteps, and I heard him fidgeting about in the study. I sat under the row of family portraits. The previous generations stared out from their frames; it was as though they competed in sternness, demanding a continuation from the subsequent generations.

Oppressive, for me, and perhaps precisely the reason why Boet had rebelled against the pre-ordained pattern that his blood forced him into.

I had arrived the previous day for my annual visit to my widower Uncle Isaac and his only son, Boet. Boet, the crown prince. Singled out from my generation to take the reins of Zuurpoort.

A farm is like a human being – it has its moods. And

Zuurpoort was depressed; I could feel it the moment I arrived. The gate hung crooked on its hinges and dragged over the road. A dragging gate is the first sign of sloppy farming. And Uncle Isaac, schooled in the traditions and disciplines of his ancestors, was not a sloppy farmer. He controlled the family heritage with a firm and tidy hand.

The second sign that things were sliding was slack boundary fences. En route to the Zuurpoort homestead, along the winding, rutted road, I noted slack wires in the fence here and there.

Uncle Isaac had opened the front door himself, standing in the dim interior of the house.

'Hello, Jac,' he said, his calloused palm in my hand.

I stepped inside: the familiar floors, the high ceiling.

There was something wrong with Uncle Isaac's shoulders – he was slightly slouched. We went to sit in the living-room. A group of Leghorn hens scratched about with their rusty-red cockerel in my late aunt's rose garden in front of the house. Once, this would have been unheard of. Fowls in the rose garden!

The conversation took its normal course: questions about how the family was doing. 'Where's Boet?' I asked. The sacred task of continuing the line; Boet had only been out of the Grootfontein Agricultural College for a couple of years.

A shadow moved across Uncle Isaac's blue eyes.

'Boet ... has gone to the border.' He bit the sentence off, his tone of voice forbidding further questions.

Nevertheless, I asked, 'But hasn't he already done his army service?'

Uncle Isaac shuffled his feet; an ornament in the glass-fronted cabinet tinkled against another. 'Boet has signed up permanently.' He got up and went out, his footsteps in the passage indicating clearly that he did not wish to discuss the matter further.

I thought about the sagging gate, the slack wires, the fowls in the elegant rose garden that had been planted and nurtured by generations of farmers' wives. The rose garden that was to be maintained in readiness for the wife that Boet would bring to Zuurpoort.

I took a candlestick to the guest room. Night had fallen on Zuurpoort. My shadow flickered black against the walls as I undressed. I lay down for a few moments, and then dropped off to sleep, the faces of ancestors flitting in and out of my dreams.

All was not well with Zuurpoort, and I sensed something of the same sickness in Uncle Isaac's voice when he took me to see the rams next morning. After the reading of the family tree, this was the second ritual of my visits.

Slowly, we rode down the field in the pick-up. The rams were grazing in small groups, some wearing canvas coats to protect the fleece. Uncle Isaac pulled up and got out, taking a handful of maize from the sack on the back of the truck.

One by one the rams approached, and I could smell the heady fragrance of lanoline. Heavy testicles swayed between rear legs, hanging like the pendulum of the old heirloom clock in the parlour at Zuurpoort.

They took the maize from Uncle Isaac's hand. Enthusiastically he pointed out conformation: 'Look at the head, the shape of the horn. The straight back, the shanks, the angle of the horns.' I had to hold one, although it was hardly necessary because the animal was too arrogant to be unruly. Uncle Isaac parted the fleece, his hands moving with practised ease over the ram's body. The grey top wool parted to reveal the white within. I had the ram by the horns and he shook his head, playfully testing my grip.

We climbed back into the pick-up and drove home.

'The old one', said Uncle Isaac, 'was South African Grand Champion three times in succession. I always only showed him at Bloemfontein and Ermelo. Now he's past it, his seed has become weak. But I keep him because he's got dignity. He lends a tone to the other rams. Did you see how he butted?'

I stood at the heart of Zuurpoort. The four-poster bed had come from the Boland with one of the ancestors. Uncle Isaac had slept alone in it since my aunt's death eight years earlier. 'A slick fellow from the Cape', Uncle Isaac once told me, 'arrived here one day and offered me a thousand for the bed. I set the dogs on him.'

How many of my grandmothers – Grandma Geertruida, Grandma Sophia, Grandma Magdalena, Grandma Martha, Grandma Magtilt – had not rocked gasping on those soft feathers to perpetuate the line of succession?

There the next generation was conceived and born; a doctor had to hurry over the forty miles from town. How many had lost their virginity and discovered motherhood here, and affirmed that motherhood again and again …

Suddenly the room seemed musty, sour. Generations stirred: my grandfather took hold of my grandmother and tore her crinoline off. She whinnied with pleasure.

My return to Zuurpoort every year was always a kind of pilgrimage, even when I was still too young to recognise it as such. You make pilgrimages to your old homes, the places where you played as a child, your school, sometimes even the room where you were born.

My visits to Zuurpoort were visits to my blood.

But this time something was wrong. I wandered round the farmyard and found signs of neglect everywhere. As the Jerseys grazed in the pasture, their ears twitched persistently – ticks. In the workshop the tools did not hang oiled and neatly arrayed as usual. And, even harder to understand, there were no servants in the house. Uncle Isaac prepared the meals himself, his big hands clumsy amongst the pots on the stove. Once or twice I came upon him with a broom, and I got out of the way, embarrassed for him.

Boet's name was not mentioned. Then at last I looked directly at Uncle Isaac who was eating with his head bowed over his food. 'Uncle Isaac,' I began. He looked up, he'd been expecting my question. 'What happened?'

He took me to the slaughter shed. Hanging there to dry was a salted sheep's hide.

'She was one of the best,' he said, 'one of my finest ewes.' He fingered the hide. 'But she didn't breed true; three seasons in succession she dropped imperfect lambs. It's strange, isn't it, how the blood has its ways.'

And then, with a gruff voice and eyes on the ground, he began to speak.

In the small hours I awoke in the guest room, frightened, drenched with sweat. I sat upright, surrounded by the shadowy forms of the furniture. The nightmare that had awoken me was still with me:

Our stroll becomes a guided tour. Uncle Isaac is feverish; his hands tremble. He unlocks the door to the trophy room. Certificates from ram shows all over the country hang on the walls. Photographs of champion rams, wool auctions. A breeders' convention in Australia, Uncle Isaac as a young man with Grandpa Johann, rigged out in the style of the time.

'Look, look,' gestures Uncle Isaac. 'Your grandfather at the ram auction in Bloemfontein. Look, there he is during the wool boom when Zuurpoort's wool prices scored a world record, Jac, a world record. Everything went in tax, almost everything.'

And in a corner, stuffed and mounted on a pedestal, with the cold glass eyes that betray the absence of life, stands the patriarch of the Zuurpoort stud.

One of Australia's top rams, imported by my ancestor, preserved for posterity.

I want to get away; the stud pins me down.

But I have to go onto the stoep to join Uncle Isaac, my late Aunt, Grandfather Johann, Grandma Magtilt, Great-grandfather Isaac, Great-grandma Margaretha.

The ram comes walking onto the front verandah, his handsome head held high in pride and his eyes fixed on the white-capped housemaid who serves tea to the family on the veranda.

'Where is Boet?' asks Aunt.

'I can hear someone coming,' says Grandma Magtilt. 'It's probably him.'

I am the only one sitting, so I can see that the footsteps are not Boet's but the tread of the patriarch ram of the Zuurpoort stud. The ram's yellow eyes gaze salaciously at the servant's legs, and when she goes inside with the empty tray, he snorts through dilated nostrils and follows her into the Zuurpoort homestead.

I excuse myself and go inside. Then I am standing before the four-poster, looking into the servant's terrified face.

I tried to shake the dream off, saw a sliver of light under my door. I pushed the door open. The light was coming from the kitchen.

In the kitchen a fire was roaring in the range. A red-hot pot hook was sticking out of the open oven door.

'Uncle Isaac?'

'Go back to sleep, Jac.' Three kettles of water steamed on the stove.

Uncle Isaac stood wearily over the stove, stubble on his cheeks.

I remembered how he'd spoken, beside the salted sheep's hide over the wire.

'I'll make coffee,' I said. Briefly his eyes blazed into

mine. They were surprisingly blue. How his ancestors must have been talking to him recently!

He took a bowl of hot water to the back door; one of the farm labourers appeared in the light and took it from him.

I fetched two mugs from the shelf, threw some coffee grounds into the pot, poured boiling water over them, and at four o'clock in the morning in the Zuurpoort farmhouse, while we sipped from our mugs, Uncle Isaac and I, respectively seven and eight generations removed from the patriarch, waited to see if the baby would have blue eyes or not.

Stubby Hands

'Come,' said the safari suit, moving to the cupboard in the corner of the classroom. The safari suit knew he didn't like maths; took out the thin yellow cane. It grated against the cupboard door. x=x; so what?

He got up from his desk, his hands sweating.

Maths is an irrelevant language, the shuffle of empty signs.

He stepped up to the table. The smell of chalk hung around the blackboard

'Bend over.'

Maths stank of chalk and the sour smell of school benches. It scrabbled with the safari suit's crooked writing on the blackboard.

He knew how he looked to the others at their desks: comical, with his head near his shins, elbows against his kneecaps, grey school pants stretched tight over his bum.

Whack. Wasn't there something wrong about making x equal to y and then proving it? Whack. Pain comes from nerves. Tell your nerves to lie. Whack. Soon you felt bugger all. Whack. It always worked. He said to himself: Lie, bum nerves, lie. Whack.

'Right.' Four. Only four. Hmph.

The thin cane was stowed away. The cupboard locked. His bench creaked as he sat down.

This morning with the group at the dam. *Ploops, ploops,* they threw pebbles into the water. *Ploops* fell the prayers in the wide dam of God's eye.

He'd planned to do his maths homework after the meeting. But then the Spirit came over their group and he was nearly late for school. He missed the school bus and had to race along on his bike. He had only just made it to the bicycle rack by the time the siren on the school hall started to wail. In a flash he was in the classroom, the classroom where the blackboard was so nice and clean in the mornings.

But in no time characters scrabbled about all over it. Spiders weaving webs in his brain. Woven in until he writhed like a caterpillar in a cocoon. No air. So muggy. Whack, whack – Sir was caning Uiltjie too. This morning at the dam Uiltjie had prayed: Dear Lord, bless our school ... and inside the cocoon you could hardly move. And it was stuffy. And the sour stench of years of sandwiches, half-rotten apples, sweaty hands and ink rose from the school bench.

At the top left on just about the only vacant spot on the surface of the desk, he had carved his initials with his compass. 1970. R.I.R. To the right under his own name: 1921. T.d.T., and: 1947. S.v.H. and P.v.d.M. 1915. And Peet van der Merwe, who had sat in this desk in 1915, his name was on the roll of honour of old boys who had fallen in the War. There his initials would remain until the siren announced break-time. Until the weekend, until the December holidays, until the Second Coming for that matter ...

'Riaan.'

If the teacher wasn't so dedicated, so conservative and dreadfully grey in his safari suit, he might have thought: You are Satan, you with your godless formulas. You with your long yellow cane. Your red insatiable ballpoint. Your chalk. Your yellow Volksie in front of the school building. Your system. You pig. You bloody bully.

'Riaan.'

Sir stood over him and looked through narrowed eyes at the small figures he'd doodled between the diagrams in his maths book. Jesus on the cross. Ripples on the surface of the dam. A Volkswagen smashed into a wall. He'd always been good at drawing.

'Riaan.'

He couldn't be caned twice in one hour's lesson. Shame on you, safari suit.

Beyond the windows, poplar trees clapped their hands. Jesus saves, Jesus saves. He had put the sticker on his suitcase. Jesus is Lord. Teachers gave it cynical glances as he walked past in the school corridors. He knew they shook their heads over it. And in his report they wrote remarks about the difference between his I.Q. and his actual performance. Lacks direction, was the common refrain.

The safari suit leant over him. He smelt of shaving cream. The teacher's face was close, too close. He could smell his skin.

His homework book lay open before him, incomplete theorems creeping over the pages, gaps in-between. Oh, Lord.

The wind whistled outside. Oh, the fragrance of the Eerste River. As sweet as the earth and water and palmiet. As sweet as a girl. The river was a woman's silver arm. Absurd.

'Riaan ...'

Buzz off, Sir. This morning Jesus came over the water, sandals on his feet, his face radiant. And Uiltjie, who you caned just now, still prayed: O Lord, bless the Paul Roos Gymnasium and its children, and – Uiltjie got stuck there, but the Great Spirit won – and its teachers, Lord.

The safari suit sighed and moved on to gawp over other shoulders. Over the good boys' shoulders. We are one in the Spirit, we are one in the Lord ... we know that our unity will one day be restored ...

The siren wailed. Thank the Lord. They stowed their books.

'Stand,' said the safari suit. They stood.

'Good morning, class.'

'Good morning, Sir.'

Once past the blackboard, the figures scurried away. On the stoep, sunlight flooded onto his face.

He made for the bicycle rack after school. He was burning with desire. But he had held out for fifteen days.

'Hey, man!' Uiltjie fell in beside him.

'Yes.'

'Old safari hit hard today, hey?'

'He's an arsehole.'

With their school bags in front of them on the handlebars, they pedalled out through the school gates. Over the bridge and then they were in the stream of Bloemhof girls, with their white thighs that showed when the wind lifted school tunics. Oh, Lord, he was so full of lust.

And a couple of days later Sir said that he would have to come for extra lessons after school. In the flat with the Gé Korsten records. A Frik du Preez poster on the wall. Zane Grey paperbacks, *Archimedes* magazines, *Physical Fitness for Men*.

They sat side by side at the small table. He had to come for classes, the exams were close now. Work through theorems. Logs. Fractions. Coefficients.

And at a certain moment during the second lesson, Sir put his hand on his thigh.

'You are coming on nicely, Riaan.'

'Yes, Sir.' How sweetly the pigeons cooed in Jan Marais Park. Sir's hand with its blunt fingers. The short thick thumb. The small nails. You could measure a man's soul by his hands. That's what the gypsy in the caravan had said, looking at his hands and saying: You are an artist or a prophet. Believe in your vocation. Don't worry. Someone will die for your sake.

Oh, someone has already died, he wanted to rejoice.

Sir's stubby hands. Sir's fumbling hand on his thigh, his mathematical voice thick with figures and thick with, he thought later, wanting?

'I have to go, Sir.'

'You are coming on well, Riaan.'

'Goodbye, Sir.'

They met near the dam every morning at seven. It was misty there, deep in the mountain above Coetzenburg. The dam attracted the mist. The forehead of the Stellenbosch mountain scowled on high. He could hear their footsteps crunching as they approached over the gravelly dam wall, and then the dim figures appeared in the mistiness. God was so close at hand. Everything downy. Misty.

'Amen, amen,' Henry murmured.

They all bought the new paperback *Good News*. Jesus was so real, so fresh. With the guitar they sang: He made the stars to shine; I've got the joy bells in my heart; Everybody ought to know …

'No wait, Sir,' he said nervously, the shallow breath near his ear, the blunt fingers feverishly clasping his thigh.

But it was only once he was outside, past the pigeons in the park, that he could say it: He's a queer!

In the afternoons the safari suit was swopped for a rugby jersey. And then they were driven over the field, backwards and forwards. Down, back, bend, stretch, open, close, in, sang the rugby jersey. 'Come on, Riaan, you're just as useless here as you are in maths. Come on, Riaan.'

But after that afternoon in the flat, Sir never came to lean over him in class again. The safari suit avoided his eyes. He was free. Sir's blunt hands had freed him from homework, from the yellow cane, from staying afterwards for extra rugby practice.

And one day Sir said, as they filed out past the board, 'Riaan, stay behind a minute, please.'

They were alone in the classroom. The smell of blackboard chalk. Sir's fingertips white with chalk. Outside the standard sixes cheered and ran for the bus or the bicycle rack.

'Riaan ...'

The safari suit wanted to see him. Over the weekend. Stuttering, he said he wanted to talk to him. He remembered the aftershave smell, the hand. After rugby practice Sir always showered with them.

The thin yellow cane: the pleasure of the safari suit.

All right, Sir. We can meet early tomorrow morning. At seven, at the dam?

What about Saturday evening at the flat?

No, he lied, they were going away for the rest of the weekend.

Fine, Riaan, at the dam on Saturday morning at seven.

He left the classroom. The bicycle rack was already empty. Only his black fat-tyred bike. Bloemhof's stream of girls had already passed. The white kneecaps, the inner thighs. In a way he could understand Sir's blunt hand. It was now thirty-two days since Henry had told the group that it was a sin. So he kept it in. In the afternoons it burnt in his throat. Then he went to the mountain road and ran until he was numb.

Tomorrow morning at seven at the dam. He grinned. Theorems and logs, yellow cane. Everybody must meet the Lord face to face.

Early, earlier than usual, he was sitting at the dam. The wind teased gently at the mist over the water. Henry came out of the mist, his three Bibles under his arm. Uil. Erna. Bibi. Piggy. Malcolm with his guitar slung sideways over his shoulder, his long hair tied back with a leather thong.

'We are one in the Spirit ...' they sang softly. It was holy. Somewhere in the mist, Jesus approached, heavenly joy on his face.

'Amen,' murmured Henry. As they prayed, he bent his head over his knees. Oh, Lord, please give me the strength to persevere. I want to, Lord. Help me. 'Amen,' breathed Henry. His nose between his knees, he could smell his own skin.

When he straightened and opened his eyes, Sir, white in the face, was standing right near them. His jaw had dropped in surprise.

'Praise the Lord,' said Henry.

'Riaan ...?' said Sir's eyes, and his stubby hands clutched at one another.

Joshua

They said he made you blow on the back of your hand to see if your balls came up. If they didn't, there was something wrong.

In the playground, the children danced in a circle round Fred Gouws. 'His balls won't come up, his balls won't come up,' they chanted.

Fred spun round and round. 'Isn't, isn't, isn't!' he said and then he had one of his attacks, freezing for a moment with his eyes fixed blindly on the ground. They pranced around him shouting, 'Wake up, Fred. Wake up, Fred.'

The school doctor used the office next door to the headmaster's. Normally it was the duplicating room and when you walked past you could hear the *slap-slap* of the copying machine. But once a year, when the school doctor came, the machine was pushed into a corner and all the children, two or three at a time, class by class, had to line up at his door. First the boys, then the girls. And each one smelt slightly of medicine when he or she came back to the classroom. When a chap came back and sat down, his pals whispered quietly so the teacher wouldn't hear: 'Did your balls come up? Did your balls come up?' Then he'd nod importantly and a paper aeroplane would sail overhead, white as a dove, to dive into a corner.

We didn't know what to ask the girls. But, like us, they had something to giggle about.

I stood pressed up against the brick wall; it was summery outside and the coolness of the red bricks was pleasant. Three of us had been called out. Me, Little Pierre and

Mad Fred for the second time. Mad Fred was in with the doctor now. I could just about make out the sound of their voices through the wall. Little Pierre waited behind me. We hadn't had break yet and he smelt of soap. We didn't say anything to each other.

Then Fred came out, his eyes staring.

'Mad Fred,' said Little Pierre.

It was my turn to go into the white place.

'Close the door.' Huge and pale, like a frog from the quarry dam, the doctor sat behind the desk. He didn't look up at me, just sat writing with his great white paw. Then he sighed and said, 'Come here, this side of the table.' I edged round and stood a little way from him. When he'd finished writing and swivelled round – *squeak, squeak* went the chair – to look at me, it seemed as though someone had opened a bottle of medicine. He breathed all over me as he looked at me. My heart beat frantically. He was going to pull my pants down.

Would my balls come up? What if I was like Fred?

'Hmmm.'

His big white hands were on me, soft as a frog's belly. He drew me closer, studying me over the top of his spectacles. I could smell him – a horrible combination of cough mixture and castor oil.

I wanted to run away. There were papers on the desk, shiny things, a silver spoon. An injection syringe!

'Joshua, is it?'

I nodded, trying to swallow the lump in my throat.

The hands felt me. 'What does your father do, Joshua?' he asked, and put the ends of the thing round his neck into his ears. He unbuttoned my shirt, but how could he hear anything? The shiny thing moved about on my chest as I answered, 'He's a stoker.'

'Hmmm.' But I knew he hadn't heard me. Those things were still in his ears. He moved the shiny thing about on my chest some more and told me, 'Breathe in, big breath.' I breathed in the smell of Dettol and everything. His breath too, warm right on my face. 'Out.' I breathed out. 'In.' In. 'Out.' Out. I was starting to feel light-headed.

'Hmmm.' He swung round on his chair again and wrote something on one of the papers on his desk.

Now he would pull my pants down. I could feel everything shrinking, fear making it all smaller.

'Mouth open.' The stubby white fingers were on my face, the one hand closed one of my eyes, the fingers of the other hand were salty against my lips.

'Hmmm.' He wrote again.

'Do you ever brush your teeth?'

I looked up quickly, but didn't answer. There was no money for toothpaste. In the morning I took the night taste out of my mouth with bread dunked in my coffee. Just as good as toothpaste. We did have toothpaste once. It tasted as nice as sweets – like peppermints. And there were little red stripes in the white worm.

He was closer now, his hand on my scalp. He didn't say anything although he wanted to. He kept quiet.

Then, 'Just pull down your pants.' He swivelled away from me to write again, his back broad and white, his big belly quivering like a frog's on the bank of the quarry dam.

'Get on with it, we haven't got all day.'

With frozen fingers I fiddled with my fly. My pants fell down round my ankles. Right over my knees, as though I was shedding a skin.

The chair squeaked. He bent over me, hooking a finger in the elastic of my underpants and pulling them away from me. As he bent and peered, I could see the pink flesh on the back of his neck with sweat glistening in the folds.

'Hmmm.' Down below, I shrank up and I got gooseflesh on my arms. What if I was like Mad Fred and the children danced around me singing, 'Joshua's balls won't come up, won't come up ...'

The big hand took hold of me. I shrank back. The hand was warm on me.

'Put your mouth against your hand.' He demonstrated. 'Now blow as hard as you can.'

I blew with all my might; I blew until my chest hurt and my head rang. The blood pounded in my ears.

The elastic snapped back against my stomach.

'Get dressed.'

I wanted to cry. Tears stung my eyes. I hadn't felt anything coming up. That morning before school I'd stood in the cloakroom and blown and I'd felt it. Now I couldn't feel anything.

'Hmmm.' He wrote. My pants were up and I tucked my shirt in shakily. He put his pen down, folded his heavy hands and looked over the desk at me. He was going to tell me something. I waited with baited breath.

'You must tell your mother to wash your hair more often.' My knees felt weak. 'You've got little ... little lice in your hair. You must wash your hair. Hmmm. You'll infect the other children. Hmmm. Listen, I'm going for tea now but if you wait for me outside I'll give you something for your head. I've got something for you in my car.' I nodded, and got out of there as fast as I could. To be outside again – to see the school quad with the little fountains and their bright jets of water, the green grass and Little Pierre, who was waiting for his turn to go in!

The doctor loomed large and white in the doorway. 'I'll be back just now,' he told us. We stood against the brick wall from where we had a good view of the teachers as they went into the staff room.

Once the doctor was out of ear-shot, Little Pierre asked me, 'What happened? Why do you have to wait?'

Suddenly I felt ashamed about my hair. Little Pierre was one of the rich boys. His father had a farm in the valley. He smelt of soap and his hair was always neatly combed and lay flat.

'Oh, he just wants to give me some cough mixture,' I lied.

Little Pierre and I never talked to each other. He was the class captain and he sat right in front. I sat at the back with the other children from Rusoord: Hermanus, Riempies and Knackers. We sat near the window and we could watch the gardener weeding the school garden. We could watch the pigeons when they came down to pick up the crumbs after break.

After a short while Little Pierre asked as if he didn't really want to know, 'Did you have to blow on your hand?' I nodded.

He looked me up and down with some interest. His eyes asked, What happened?

I could feel the cold brick wall against my body. 'Did it work?' Little Pierre asked, looking away from me at the shiny fountain.

'Came up just so high,' I said, showing him with my fingers. He looked at me with wide eyes. 'With the very first blow,' I added for good measure.

Little Pierre half turned away from me with his hands behind his back. He leaned against the wall. There was a small crease between his eyebrows.

Then the doctor came back and gave me a packet with a bottle in it. 'Use it twice a week,' he breathed at me. He went inside with Little Pierre trailing behind him. As soon as the door shut, I shot off to the cloakroom.

At the urinal I put my packet on the floor and pulled down my pants and underpants. With my one hand under my balls, I blew on the other hand. I felt the little sacks tense, they stirred, lifted slightly and then up they came.

I peed a golden-yellow streak, the highest yet – high against the back of the urinal, almost on a level with my nose. Satisfied, I went back through the white sunlight to my class. It was only when I was back in my desk that I remembered the stuff to wash my hair with – I'd left it in the cloakroom.

Pa was out stoking – to Noupoort. Ma put her lace-up shoes on – she smelt of bean soup – and shut the door behind her.

Riempies hung onto the garden gate, panting, his fingers weaving in and out of the rusty wire. 'Aunty, aunty, aunty,' he kept saying as he followed her down the dirt road. I went with them, walking in the fine red powdery dust of Rusoord's roads that sucked your feet in, warm liquid dust. My feet were tough and, anyway, we weren't in a hurry.

We Rusoord children were too poor to pay the ten cents they asked at the town swimming pool. After school every afternoon we went for a dip in the quarry dam up on the hill behind Rusoord. When the road workers had finished quarrying there, they'd fenced it and put up a lot of skull-and-crossbones signs. Danger. But we made a hole in the fence and got through to swim naked, squabbling with the children from the location when they showed up too.

My little brother Jacob bunked school – he was no good at sums – and went to the quarry dam by himself in the afternoon. Riempies had appeared out of breath at our door.

'Aunty, aunty, aunty,' he kept saying until we were up on the hill.

My mother didn't say anything.

The police walked all round the dam with their long hooks. The water was as black as ironstone. They dragged deep. One hook caught, came loose, caught again, mud clouded the black water, my eyes misted over ... the policeman's arms ... he tugged ... then everything round me was clouded.

I fell face forward onto the wet rocks.

And in all that time my mother didn't say anything.

My father was at Noupoort, out stoking.

On Monday morning all the children from Rusoord and from the railway camp on the other side of the line were called to old Fishy's office. We stood in a long line and each of us got a piece of cheese, a mug of milk and a spoonful of cod-liver oil.

Riempies and Hermanus nudged me.

'Say you're sad, you want more cheese.'

It was a good idea, but I didn't feel like it. Jacob hadn't been dead a week and we were still mourning.

'Go on. Go on.' Riempies nudged me again

'Ag, man.' The milk was rich and creamy, the cheese turned into porridge as you chewed it. Then the cod-liver oil. It was revolting. You kept it in your cheek and then spat it out as you passed the fountains on the way back to your classroom.

'Joshua, stay behind, please,' said old Fishy. 'The headmaster wants a word with you.' I nearly jumped out of my skin. Mamba, our headmaster, had a tongue that flickered over his lips the whole time, just like a snake's tongue does. He strikes when he hits you, he hits when he strikes, the children chanted.

'Oh, shit,' Knackers said to me, 'what have you done now?' I shrugged.

'His brother is dead,' Hermanus said.

They hung about, hands in their pockets. It was always bad if the headmaster wanted to see you.

Then, 'I suppose we'd better go,' they said.

'Okay.'

They went off, spitting as they passed the fountain even though they'd swallowed the cod-liver oil a while ago.

'Joshua,' said old Mamba. I checked quickly to see if his cane was leaning against the cupboard. It wasn't.

'Joshua,' he said again, 'Miss Brouwer and I thought it might be a good thing for you to spend a bit of time on a farm.' The tongue flickered out, leaving a shiny streak on his lower lip before it disappeared again. 'Your mother was very shocked by little Jacob's death. Perhaps it would be a good thing for you to go away to a farm for your week-ends.'

He was watching me closely. I tried to keep an eye on his right hand but it was out of sight behind a pile of books. They said his hand was the size of a plate. Some-times he hit the children – especially the small ones – with an open hand. And he left red finger-marks right over the whole backside.

'Look,' Jacob had said one day, 'old Mamba's hand covered my whole bum.' He showed us in the cloakroom. Mamba could draw blood.

'Joshua, do you know Little Pierre?'

I nodded. Little Pierre got stars for good work every day, and after school his mother was always waiting for him at the gate in a Dodge. The Dodge had huge tail-fins like the sails on a windmill.

'Did you know that his father is the chairman of the school committee?'

I shook my head. No, I didn't know that. I just knew that his father had a foreman. They farmed in the valley. And every year Little Pierre's father slaughtered three sheep for our class stall at the school fête and then we won easily. And every year Little Pierre received the cup for the best stall because he was class captain.

'Mr Jordaan says that Little Pierre is going to invite you to come home with him to the farm for the weekends.'

But, sir, I wanted to say, Little Pierre never even talks to me. We never play together. We're not friends.

'So, is that settled then, Joshua?' I didn't say anything, I just stared at the knobs on the intercom at Mamba's elbow.

'Joshua?'

'Yes, sir,' I said quietly.

Mamba stood up. He looked even taller than he did on Fridays on the stage in the hall.

'It'll be nice on the farm, Joshua,' he said. 'There'll be lots of things there you won't have come across before.'

I went out. At the fountain, I stopped. The stream of water broke up in the air and fell like diamonds. The cod-liver oil was bitter in my cheek. Pa was on the way to Noupoort when Jacob drowned.

'My child has drowned,' Pa said when he came back from stoking. 'Drowned like a rat in a gravel pit.' And he drank and he cried and later he lay on the bed and snored, on his back, his mouth open, the stubble blue on his cheeks.

I thought about the Dodge with the tail-fins and the way it purred off every day with Little Pierre sitting in front next to his mother. And I thought about the doctor's soft hands, the way my balls came up, the brown packet and the stuff to wash my hair with.

'Don't you ever brush your teeth?' the doctor had asked.

Outside on the playground, Mad Fred was turning round and round crazily, his eyes fixed on the ground as the children round him chanted, 'His balls won't come up, his balls won't come up.'

Friday came as all Fridays do. I was dreading Friday and the Dodge.

Ever since old Mamba had called me in, I'd kept an eye on Little Pierre. He sat a long way away from me in class and he was always quick to jump and clean the board or run an errand for a teacher. He never looked at me but I couldn't take my eyes off the back of his head.

'He doesn't even want to play with you,' Knackers said. 'Why do you want to go and stay with the rich people?'

'You'll have to wear a tie for breakfast,' teased Hermanus.

'Mustn't spit.'

'Can't swim with nothing on.'

'Mustn't smoke.'

'Comb your hair just like Little Pierre.'

'You not allowed to spit, you not allowed to spit …' they mocked. Hermanus had picked up a used matchstick and dug in his ear with it.

'You've got lice again,' said Riempies.

'Head lice don't go into a your ears,' Hermanus argued.

'Oh yes, they do.'

'Don't.'

'They do. They eat your head away from the inside.'

'That must be why I can't do sums,' crowed Hermanus, leaping on to Riempies for a rough and tumble that lasted until Riempies's nose started to bleed. Then the bell rang and Little Pierre had to make sure that we lined up neatly. They nudged me.

'Say hello to your buddy.'

'Bugger off, man.'

'You not allowed to swear, you not allowed to swear.' Hermanus and Knackers murmured their song all the way to our classroom.

And in the classroom there was the back of Little Pierre's head and Friday afternoon getting closer and closer.

I leant against the wall at the back trying to think up an opening sentence for my composition and longing for Jacob, my dead brother with the bony knees.

'Class rise.'

We stood up and filed out, row by row, Little Pierre leading. The Dodge was waiting at the gate. My hand was so sweaty I could hardly hold my case. My heart beat worse than it had at the doctor's.

Hermanus, Riempies and Knackers were hanging around under the pepper trees. I tried to pretend I hadn't seen them. Riempies hopped up and down to attract my attention, but I kept my eyes to the front. Little Pierre had already got to the Dodge. He put his case in the boot. His father got out and came to meet me.

'You must be Joshua,' he said and his hand was warm over mine. He squatted down in front of me and said, 'We're going to make you into a farmer.' His forehead was very white and he was big and friendly.

Little Pierre stood sulkily near one of the Dodge's tail-fins. I nodded to him.

'Come on, chaps,' said his father. I got into the back of the Dodge. It was bigger than I'd realised. I could only just reach to see through the window. The glass was blue-ish, like sunglasses.

As we drove off, I looked back. Hermanus and Riempies and Knackers waited near the pepper trees, their socks sagging round their ankles, their legs suddenly looking as thin as sticks.

They were my buddies. I badly wanted to be with them.

The Dodge seemed to be bigger than the houses in Rusoord. We had to collect my clothes, and I hoped Pa wouldn't be there with his blue stubble and red eyes and the sour wine smell on his breath. Perhaps Ma would also be out. I was ashamed, and I prayed. Little Pierre's father was talking but I didn't take in a word. Children and fowls scattered before the Dodge's bumper and all the aunties came out inquisitively, leaning their thick soup arms on their gates.

'Which way now, Joshua?' I pointed. My voice sounded faint even in my own ears. Little Pierre kept quiet but his neck was as stiff as a ramrod.

We stopped in front of our house and I jumped out. The gate was dragging again, the hinge was broken again. Simon sniffed my ankles and lifted a leg to pee against the Dodge tyre before I could stop him. Little Pierre's father laughed. 'It doesn't matter – the farm dogs do that too.'

Ma and Pa came out. I watched Little Pierre's father. They introduced themselves. Pa wasn't drunk. Ma was wearing the funeral dress she'd bought for Jacob. They chatted and Little Pierre's father laughed heartily. Pa was scratching his elbows and Ma was smoothing down her dress the whole time.

'Thank you, Mr Jordaan. Thank you, Mr Jordaan, sir,' Ma said.

With my bundle of clothes on my knee we were off. Simon came back to the tyre. Pa shooed him away too fiercely. I had climbed into the car, but Ma said, 'Don't you say goodbye?' Embarrassed, I got out again and kissed her. 'Remember the manners we've taught you,' she said, but not really to me – more to Little Pierre's father. Pa took my hand. His eyes were moody. He actually looked as though he was going to lash out at me.

We drove off.

Little Pierre didn't say anything all the way to the farm. The Dodge swung off the tar road and the gravel of the dirt road ground under its belly. It was low-slung, like a ship in the water or a wire car with strips of car-tube for springs.

There was a signboard: Wildehoek. The house stood between the trees, white as an iced cake.

'Right,' said Little Pierre's father as we drew up in the garage and the cool darkness folded about us. I didn't want to get out. I thought about Pa wobbling along Rusoord's dusty streets on his old bone-shaker bicycle, his lunch-tin clipped onto the carrier behind him and the wildness in his eyes.

'The fire is eating me, woman,' he would tell Ma. It's hell, he said, to stoke through the Karoo to Noupoort and then back again. Or sometimes to De Aar, where all the trains in the world meet and wait on tracks that branch out like the veins on a leaf.

'Come on, Joshua.' We walked past the lines of rose bushes and the nozzles that sprayed water over everything, the green grass that curved up into little mounds and dipped into little hollows like the church garden. Two Great Danes which I'd heard Little Pierre talking about, came lolloping up, spit dripping from their black mouths, with those pink gums. I wanted to leave, to go back onto the gravel road, then the tarred road, then turn off at Rusoord and sit with Ma, watching her stir the green soup.

'Don't you ever brush your teeth?' the white hands had asked.

Little Pierre's father put his hand on my shoulder and then we'd crossed the deep stoep and were in the house. It was cool and dark inside. Quiet. A long passage with paintings on the walls and a sitting-room with a fireplace, a thick carpet that sucked your feet in like dust, and deep chairs. Through another room that also looked like a sitting-room, except the chairs weren't as nice as the ones in the first room. Then over a floor that was so shiny that I could see my shins and my knee-caps reflected in it.

'You've got bandy legs,' Riempies always told me. 'You'll never be able to catch a pig.'

Past a dining-table probably big enough for twenty people and then down a long passage to a room that smelt as though it was kept shut up. The window was open and I could see the dogs running about like calves on the lawn, but the room smelt musty.

'This is your room,' Little Pierre said. It was the first thing he'd said to me. I put my clothes on the bed. Outside the nozzles sprayed water out in shiny jets.

'So this is Joshua, is it?' She was pretty – I had seen her driving away from school in the Dodge every day. Her arms were covered with flour up to the elbows.

'I can't shake your hand,' she laughed. 'I'm baking some special rusks for the weekend.'

She showed me the cupboard and asked if I slept with one or two pillows. I shrugged and scratched my elbows just like Pa and asked quietly, 'Where is the bathroom?'

I wanted to escape from Little Pierre's watchful eyes, from his father who stood smiling behind the woman in the doorway, the woman who asked about pillows and talked about rusks. I stood amongst the white tiles and I wanted to cry, but I held it in, breathing quickly for a few minutes. They were probably waiting for me. I pushed the shiny knob to flush the pan so they'd think that I'd used it. I was dreading the meals. To sit at that big table and not to know how to hold your fork. To feel the eyes on you. Not to know how to answer if they asked you about Pa's work.

I opened the door and went out into the passage, realised I was going in the wrong direction, turned quickly in the dim passage and reached a room I hadn't been in before. Books right up to the ceiling and a huge desk covered with papers. I hurried back into the passage with my heart jumping frantically in my throat. I turned left and crossed another room and in the distance I could make out the sound of voices and the clink of crockery. Unable to breathe, I tried to remember. I couldn't call out, what would they think of me? I turned round again and almost walked into a huge portrait of a man who stared at me with wild, angry eyes. Somewhere a clock started to chime, the voices were further away now, the house was big and dark.

In the dimness of a back room, I started to cry quietly.

We ate at the big table; four people at the one polished end. I wasn't very hungry.

'Why don't you two go down to the river with the air-gun, Little Pierre?'

'All right, Dad.'

Little Pierre didn't want me here. How could we be buddies? I belonged with Hermanus and Riempies and Knackers, standing under the pepper trees with their thin legs.

We finished eating, pudding and coffee in tiny cups. Little Pierre pushed back his chair. 'Come on,' he said.

'Excuse me.' Perhaps they wouldn't see the bits of rice near my plate. And on the tablecloth a little way from my plate, a green pea. I wanted to pick it up, but their eyes were on me. We got up to go, one meal was behind me, the airgun stood in the corner and we counted out the pellets, as grey as the gravel pebbles in the quarry dam.

'If you don't count them out,' Little Pierre said, 'you can shoot off a whole packet of five hundred without realising you're doing it.'

'Oh.' I scratched my elbows. Aeroplanes hung on fishing line from the ceiling. They flew gently in the breeze from the open window – a squadron against a white cloud of ceiling.

'I made them myself.' Little Pierre took one down, the chair wobbling under his weight and me trying to hold it steady. 'Look, the guns turn.'

Then we were outside. The dogs must have smelt food on me because they kept nearly knocking me head over heels. Their big soft paws. Spit on my arm. 'Get away! Get away!'

Two peacocks strutted away on the lawn, hundreds of bees buzzed near the lower garden gate.

'We must run past here,' Little Pierre said, 'otherwise the swarm will mob us.' We ran with the shadows of the dogs splashing black onto the path, pink tongues dripping spit, sunshine warm on the neck.

Out in the open, away from the shadowy house, I felt better.

Little Pierre was talking to me. The dogs were clumsy and lovable and all over the place – under our feet, ahead on the path, half down an old antbear hole or barking after something.

'This is a nice farm,' I said. Little Pierre nodded proudly.

'It's my father's,' he said unnecessarily, and I was a bit cheesed off about that.

We went down to the river, through the strong smell of wet soil in the dongas. The dogs were quieter now; noses on the ground, they disappeared into the reeds, their clumsy bodies rustling and thrashing about. Then suddenly we came upon a clearing with water and a sandbank. The dogs were gone, the water drifted lazily past. Only an ant, rowing desperately with its tiny legs, showed that the water was moving at all.

'You don't want me here,' I said to Little Pierre. He glanced at me, churned up the sand with one foot, then shoved the butt of the airgun into the sand so it stood upright.

'We're not friends,' he said, but there was nothing ugly in his eyes.

'Old Mamba said I had to come.'

He nodded. 'Because of Jacob.'

'Yes.' And so we stood for a moment. The ant was gone. The dogs reappeared from the reeds over the river, wet and muddy. They splashed through the water and shook themselves, showering us with drops of water and the smell of their bodies.

'Come on,' said Little Pierre. 'There are weavers' nests round the bend.'

We sat on the warm sand. Beside Little Pierre lay the limp bodies of four weavers, yellow and broken, with a little blood trickling down from their beaks into the sand. We were drenched with sweat from stalking them through the reeds, holding our breaths until the shot was fired and then charging up if the bird fluttered down into the reeds. If we wounded one we had to chase it – the injured bird flying off in fits and starts, us trying to keep up with it on the ground. Until we were close enough to shoot it dead, or the bird keeled over and dropped off the perch of its own accord.

'We can have a swim.' Little Pierre pointed to a pool near us where the river eddied against some rocks. 'It's bloody deep. Look how black the water is.' We drew nearer. 'Even the dogs won't go in here.' I thought about little Jacob and the hooks. 'You could easily drown here,' said Little Pierre.

We stripped off our clothes. The sun felt good on our skin and the water tickled like insects' feet. 'Look!' Little Pierre demonstrated that it was too deep for him to stand. When we started to get cold no one wanted to be the first out. But the water was gnawing at my legs, so I swam to the side.

We jumped up and down on the sand to dry off.

'Race you to the tree and back.' We charged off, the sand tugging at our feet, the wind cold on our skin. Out of breath, we made it back to our clothes.

Little Pierre flopped down on the sand. 'Joshua,' he said.

'Yes.'

'The school doctor …' He got stuck there.

'Yes?' I sat down too. He played with the sand.

'The children tease Mad Fred.'

'Yes.' I laughed. 'His balls won't come up.'

Little Pierre shifted uncomfortably. 'How high did yours come up?' He looked at me suddenly.

'A bit.'

'No, but how high?'

I realised he was afraid of being like Mad Fred. He was afraid like I was. I remembered how I'd showed him with my fingers outside the school doctor's door.

'Just a little bit.'

'Like this?' He showed me with his fingers.

I shook my head. 'No, not so much.'

But he still wasn't satisfied. 'Well, how much?'

I stood up. 'I'll show you.' He got up too. With our mouths to our hands we blew, naked on the sand. We blew and blew until we were both red in the face. And hardly anything happened.

Then Little Pierre shoved me playfully. I fell over, grabbed a handful of sand and chased him. Evening was coming, the starlings were chattering and, dirty from our mud fight, we went home with the dead birds and the air-gun.

Pa sat morosely sucking on his pipe. A bottle of sweet wine stood at his elbow.

'And how is Missus Jordaan?' Ma asked. She prodded me with a finger. 'Is it very grand, Joshie?'

'Ag ...' Pa blew out blue smoke between us. I could see he didn't like Ma's talk. He was tired, they'd just come in, he'd been as far as Cookhouse. Stoke, stoke, stoke, Pa always said when he came back. And the other men? Ma asked. They eventually became drivers. That meant a bigger house, on the other side of the line, with an inside lavatory and everything.

But Pa stoked, stoked, stoked. And it was driving him mad.

'And then? And then?' the other children asked. I told them about the toy aeroplanes with guns that turned. And about the big dogs chasing the peacocks. Ma pushed the pots around on the stove, Pa got up and went outside, slamming the door behind him. We heard the grating of the corrugated-iron toilet door.

'And then? And then?' asked Ma and the children.

On Monday morning Hermanus, Riempies and Knackers waited at our gate, their school bags as limp as dead birds on the ground at their feet.

'Howzit.'

'Hello.'

'How was it?'

'Ag ...'

We set off. Knackers took out his cattie and shot at everything that was shiny and made a noise. Clang went the Viljees' metal gate, clang went the jam tin on the pavement, clang went the hubcap of Big Ears's car.

'Big Ears will clout you.'

'Ha ha.'

They wanted to hear; they walked with their eyes fixed on me; they wanted me to tell them everything. 'Come, on Joshua man, tell us.'

'We shot weaver birds,' I said. 'Five.'

'What with?'

'An airgun. A Gicado.'

'Are they very rich?'

I kicked a stone. 'Yes. Their house is as big as the school.'

'You lie.'

''Strue's Bob, just as big. And rooms, one leading into another one.' I thought about getting lost and the angry eyes of the portrait. 'You could get lost there.'

'And how's old Smoothie?'

'Who?'

'Little Pierre, man.'

'Oh, him.' What could I say? That at first he didn't even want to talk to me? And later got friendly? That we were buddies down by the river but not so much in the Dodge on the way back to town?

'Ag, him.' 'I kicked another stone. They waited. 'And what did you do?' I asked.

'We hung around.' They were disappointed that I didn't have any more to tell them.

'There were big dogs,' I tried again. 'As big as calves. They eat a sheep just about every day …'

Riempies looked at me sideways.

'Was it nice, Josh?' he asked.

I thought for a minute. Was it? 'No,' I said. 'Rusoord is better.'

They looked relieved. 'Have a go with my cattie, Josh,' Knackers offered. 'I cut a new piece of car-tube for it on Saturday.' We chatted all the way to school, stamping our feet to make the dust rise on the sidewalk, taking pot-shots at the dogs with the cattie, spitting against every lamppost, then haring along the last stretch when we heard the school-bell ring.

I didn't feel good inside. It wasn't right that Hermanus and Riempies and Knackers had stayed behind.

When we were standing in line, Hermanus nudged me. 'There he is.' And he pointed to Little Pierre, who stood a little apart with the other class captains while we fell into line.

'Okay, okay,' I said. We stood to attention while *Die Stem* was played. The flag was hoisted at the other end of school; we couldn't see it, but we could hear the rope running through the pulleys.

'The flag is squeaking again today,' whispered Riempies and someone giggled. Little Pierre looked in our direction. His eyes met mine and slid away quickly.

Hermanus had a safety pin and he pricked Knackers in the bum.

'Stop it,' said Knackers crossly. The flag was still squeaking. We weren't allowed to move otherwise it was six of the best from old Mamba.

'Squeak, squeak,' whispered Riempies. Little Pierre pretended he hadn't heard. Any other day he would have come over to us. Today he looked the other way, an irritable crease between his eyes.

When the bell rang he walked down the line. He didn't look at me. The line began to move.

'Your buddy doesn't even say hello to you,' sneered Hermanus at the classroom door.

And then Pa's moodiness got the upper hand. 'The Jordaan boy must come and spend a weekend with us,' he said. It was after my fourth weekend at Little Pierre's. Pa didn't like my going.

'You're my son. I want you in my house.'

And he cornered Little Pierre's father one day when the Dodge called by to pick up my clothes. Little Pierre's father said yes straight away, but Little Pierre didn't look happy about it. For him it was all right if I came to visit on his farm, but he didn't want to come to Rusoord. He didn't want to say hullo to me at school. At the weekend we played together, we were good friends on the farm, but at school he played with his buddies and I played with Hermanus and them.

They talked about different things. They played differently. Us Rusoord boys played behind the hall where the grass wasn't cut and you could do anything you liked. And every now and then Knackers would roll a zol and we'd smoke ourselves silly and throw up in the toilets.

Now Little Pierre's father dropped us in front of the house. Little Pierre was sulking, he looked at the house as if he was seeing it for the first time. The crowd of children at the gate greeted him and he ignored them as though they weren't there.

'Voetsak, you,' I chased them away. The Dodge pulled off and I remembered getting lost in Little Pierre's house. Perhaps he also felt lost here.

'Come on, man,' I said. He dragged his heels up the steps.

'You didn't want to come,' I said. He just shrugged.

'I didn't want to go to your place either at first. But later it got better.'

He was still sulking. 'But there's a lot to do at my place. There's nothing to do here.'

'There is, there is.' I wanted to show him, to take him up the hill. 'We can climb up the hill. Us kids have built a shack with bits of corrugated-iron up there. And there's a cave on the other side of the beacon.' He'd started to pay attention. 'And there's the quarry ...' I bit my tongue. Since Jacob I had never been back there.

'Come on, show me the hill,' said Little Pierre.

We went out, sending the fowls scattering as we sprinted down the street. When we reached the first stones of the ridge we challenged each other, 'Race you!', charging up the slope so fast the skinny dog could hardly keep up.

'He's very old,' I excused him. 'He's ten years old.'

'That'd be sixty for a person.'

'No ways, it's about eighty ... or more.'

We argued for a while and then agreed that the dog was very old, even older than old Frans, who irrigated the vegetable garden on the farm.

We reached the beacon out of breath. People had scratched their names onto the white drum. I brought the nail out from under the stone. 'We keep a nail under the stone. Every time the municipality comes up here they whitewash the beacon and then we have the nail handy to write our names again.'

Little Pierre laughed and I showed him how to scratch in his name.

'Jacob's ... name they've already painted out,' I told him. 'We hoped they'd leave it. Riempies wrote a little piece nearby asking them not to paint it over, but they did.' I showed him where Jacob had written his name.

'Show me the cave,' said Little Pierre.

In the cave we imagined it went in terribly far. We explored deep into the hill, discovering treasure in the furthest corner, conquering the impi that guarded the treasure and chasing a leopard with spears until the thin dog had lost all his stuffing and nearly croaked.

We only stopped when we got to the quarry. The dog's tongue was hanging right out of his mouth. Standing close together we looked through the fence at the black water.

Then we turned down the hill to where the houses stood like boulders.

'We're poor,' I said.

'Yes,' said Little Pierre. He picked up a stone and threw it as far as he could. 'But it doesn't matter, Joshua. It's okay.'

It was Sunday evening and Pa's bottle lay on the floor, empty.

We ate the green soup.

'When is your father coming, Little Pierre?' asked Ma.

'At eight, after church.'

Pa glared at Little Pierre from under his eyebrows. 'Why do you people pray?' he asked. 'You've already got everything.'

'Barend!'

Little Pierre looked nervous. I could feel my heart shrink. Pa's shadow was huge against the wall.

We ate the green soup. I prayed that Pa wouldn't lose his temper.

'They've got everything,' Pa said again later. 'A fancy car. A farm. A big house that everyone from Rusoord would fit into. They slaughter three oxen every winter. What do they want in church?'

'Pa,' I ventured. When Pa drank, we children said nothing. And if he got violent we went to call Hermanus's father. He would come and speak to Pa and later Pa would stretch out on the sofa and go to sleep with his shoes on.

'Yes, young Josh,' said Pa. He glared at me. 'You prefer to visit them. You don't have to eat soup there.'

I could see Little Pierre was trembling. I had hoped we could be friends. I had hoped he'd enjoy it in Rusoord. I wanted to shout at Pa: drunkard, drunkard, drunkard! But I was scared of his heavy hands and his red eyes. He was mad now, ready to lash out.

Pa stood up. The children backed away, slipping out quietly because they knew what was coming. Ma tried to stop him.

'No, Bennie!' she screamed.

The empty bottle crashed to the floor. Little Pierre was sobbing now.

'Old Barend the drunk stoker!' screamed Pa. 'Old drunk Barend is not good enough for his own son.' He came towards me.

'No, Pa!' I grabbed Little Pierre's arm and we rushed out of the house. Behind us the soup pot fell to the floor. Ma was crying and the cool evening air flooded over my face. Little Pierre was ahead of me, I heard his footsteps thumping on the dirt road.

'Little Pierre,' I yelled. I was crying now too. Pa was on the stoep behind me. I ran after Little Pierre and, at the corner, near Hermanus's house, I saw the Dodge lights coming down the road. The car stopped near Little Pierre. I stood in the shadow of the fence. Little Pierre was talking to his father through the open window. Then he went round the car and got in. The Dodge swung across the road, reversed and then drove off quickly.

And so it was over.

I would never visit at Little Pierre's again, and he would never come to my place again. At school everything would go on as usual. We'd smoke behind the hall and he and his friends would talk about their aeroplanes and their pigeons.

On Monday morning in the line at school I kept my eyes down.

I didn't want to see Little Pierre.

I'd pretended I was sick that morning.

'You must go,' Ma said. 'I'll write a note to Little Pierre's father.'

And she said, 'You must take Little Pierre's clothes.' Because he'd just left them.

I shook my head.

In the class there was the back of Little Pierre's head. He didn't look round. Pa's eyes were weak that morning. He hadn't looked at me. He'd battled through the dust with the bone-shaker bicycle, then got off and pushed the bike up to the tar. Then he rode off with his chain creaking, the blackened man who worked on the blackened trains.

They were dancing round Fred Gouws again.

'Mad Fred, Mad Fred, his balls won't come up, his balls won't come up.'

Some of the girls had joined the circle although they didn't understand what was going on. Mad Fred's eyes were fixed on the girls and, as the children danced around him, he turned round and round too.

'Isn't,' he said, 'Isn't.'

I went up to them. 'Leave him alone,' I said.

They paid no attention.

'Leave him alone!' I tugged at Andries.

Mad Fred moved to one side, then he had an attack and his eyes went dead, fixed on the ground.

'Wake up, Mad Fred!' The children ran off, laughing.

Mad Fred came to and hurried crying into the toilets, looking like a galloping camel with his big body.

I followed. I remembered how frightened Little Pierre had been about his balls. And I'd also gone to the toilets afterwards to make sure.

The cloakroom stank of pee. The musty smell pressed the noise of the children back and dampened it. I saw Mad Fred's reflection in the mirrors above the wash-basins, then I came round the half-wall and found him at the urinal.

He'd dropped his pants to his ankles. His scrawny hairy legs looked ridiculous. A long thin stream hung from his one nostril. It trembled as he sobbed. Mad Fred wept, his ugly face crumpled up.

'Isn't, isn't,' he sobbed.

'Mad Fred,' I said. 'Don't worry.'

A long way away I heard the bell ringing. Mad Fred sniffed the snot in. Then he started crying and it came slithering out again.

'Joshua, Joshua.'

'Mad Fred?'

'Here, Joshua.'

Outside, the second bell rang. I knew the others were in line and now Little Pierre had them walking.

Mad Fred pulled his underpants down. Behind him were the pee-marks on the urinal. We were always seeing who could pee the highest.

'Come, Joshua.'

'Mad Fred?'

'Feel, Joshua, feel.' In the mirrors above the wash-basins I saw Mad Fred and me standing, six times over we stood.

His was big, bigger than ours, and there were long, curly hairs.

Then I felt Mad Fred's balls lying heavy and warm in my hand.

And I cried with Mad Fred, beside the white wash-basins, the mirrors, the stink of pee and, beyond the cloakroom, the empty playground with the wind stirring the sandwich-papers thrown away by laughing children.

Jan Spierewit

We who were living are now dying
With a little patience ...
T S Eliot: *The Waste Land*

At the check-in counter of the Harrismith Holiday Inn I drew the attention of my two fellow travellers to a short newspaper report that had been cut out, neatly circled with a red pen and stuck up above the visitors' book:

Further to the south-west you reach Mount QwaQwa, a flat-topped sandstone mountain inhabited by a colony of vultures. Over the centuries, their droppings have stained the cliffs white, so that even in summer they seem to be covered with snow, as they are in winter. This is how QwaQwa, which means white-white, got its name.

'Deceptive place,' I said, but the receptionist did not laugh. We signed in. No, I indicated to the receptionist, I'll sign for all three of us because these men are my responsibility. They stood hesitantly beside their bags as I filled in the register. We came from a long way off – a university in the humid hills Hendrik Verwoerd had once flown over. His eyes had ranged over the green landscape and he had said, 'I want a university here.' The prime minister's mission that day had been military rather than educational, and the flustered members of his entourage had hastened to get the longitude and latitude of the place from the pilot.

Verwoerd's 'here' had been little more than landscape; seventeen kilometres from the nearest town, with a river meandering through the hills, huts clustered like warts against the slopes, small herds of cattle, and paths as criss-crossed as the veins on a leaf. But in Verwoerd's vision it must already have looked different: immaculate faculty buildings, a glass amphitheatre, black youth at play, aspiring to the ultimate ethnic sport. And eventually, around this tree of knowledge, a republic.

We followed the porter down the corridor. The university was pampering us: we each had a bedroom with bathroom en suite. I accompanied the porter to their rooms. Mr M, the extrovert, gave his TV set a few hasty jabs, switched it on and, with the test pattern behind him, turned smilingly to me. He was short and stocky and obviously came from a very rich family of western Free State merchants. He zipped around the campus in a Citi-Golf.

Mr P, the bitter one, went straight into his bathroom, turned on the tap with the red dot and looked satisfied when hot water ran over his hand. He was lean, quiet and intense – already the archetypal ideologue. A serious student, he had made something of a name for himself in the fledgling drama school established on the campus by a brave immigrant.

I left them, each in the middle of his room on the deep-pile carpeting beside the quilt-covered double beds, surrounded by Tretchikoff prints and the soothing tones from the small speakers built into the bed's headboard.

Our trip through the night to the hotel had not been without its charge of tension. As we'd driven away from the campus late in the afternoon, a squad of policemen in fatigues were gathering beside the administration building. Flexing their long quirts, they kept an eye on the students on the opposite side of the dip. It was Steve Biko Day and the students had formed a huge ring and were dancing, stamping their feet and singing, the men in deep baritones, the women with shrill ululations. Two Casspirs waited on the sidelines, casting a shadow on a pack of highly strung Alsatians in a small trailer. At the main entrance, beside his cream Mercedes, the rector was in worried discussion with the registrar in his powder-blue safari suit.

It could not have been easy that day for my two students to drive with a white lecturer, through the gates and past the security guards with their crackling two-way radios. For the first two hours they had been withdrawn and tense, listening to the cassette that I'd slipped into the tape-player:

Through these fields of destruction
Baptisms of fire
I've watched all your suffering
As the battles raged higher …

Some day you'll return to
Your valleys and your farms
And you'll no longer burn
To be brothers in arms …

They'd only started to relax after dark, as we drove through stretches of burnt-out winter grass and I'd stopped at a café and bought hamburgers and Coke. I put the cash slip away carefully so that I could claim the small amount when I got back to the university.

We went into the dining-room, through the yakking travellers clustered round breakfast tables. The night drive had worn us out. We sat and looked about us. At this halfway station between Johannesburg and Durban, most people were dressed for what lay ahead: Gotcha, Pierre Cardin and showy Monatic. We watched as bulging buffalo-hide wallets were drawn out, credit cards slipped onto trays.

Through the window you could see the travellers under the great domed roof over the filling station. Cars jam-packed with holiday equipment drew up at the pumps. There were racquets, surfskis, beach balls, T-shirts with *Fuck Operation Hunger* and *I'm Coming!* Paunchy men kept a sharp eye on the digital readings on the pumps, and on one side an Indian family stood helplessly round a boiling car. Steam spewed out from under the bonnet.

To the other guests, I imagine we looked like three detectives, or perhaps an agricultural adviser with his two henchmen, or a speculator with his interpreters.

Our plates were piled high with egg, kidneys, kudu liver, pork sausages and grilled tomato. Yoghurt, corn flakes, glasses of yellow orange juice, cool and small in the hand with clinking ice-blocks.

At a loss, they looked at me. I shrugged. We ate in silence. We didn't know what to say.

'Do you want to deliver your speeches to me after breakfast?' I asked. Perhaps we could improvise a lectern in one of the bedrooms and simulate the evening's competition, so that they would feel more at home before the judges?

They said, no thank you, everything was under control. 'All we need is forty winks,' Mr M showed off his grasp of idiom with a naughty grin.

Later, when I was preparing to take a catnap after a tepid shower, they knocked on my door. Perhaps it would help if we had a practice run. I straightened the coverlet on the bed. The TV set, pulled away from the wall on its stand, served as lectern. They would take up their positions behind it and I would stand in for the chairman, with a pen to my lips and a score-card.

Mr M spoke on sex education at school (one of the suggested subjects). He gestured charmingly and sometimes a touch over-enthusiastically. His smile bewitched the room. When it was Mr P's turn, he gripped the TV set nervously and hunched his shoulders over his notes as though he wanted to protect the words. He did not look at us where we sat on the bed, but beyond us to the landscape of the white wall behind us. He had chosen his own subject: drama as vehicle for social change. When he was finished we clapped. He sat down again.

'That was good,' I said. 'You are both very good.'

Mr P kept his eyes cast down, Mr M looked eagerly at the score-card that I'd folded my hands over.

'Who won?' he asked. 'Who was the best?'

I shrugged. 'You're both equally good,' I said. 'It was a draw.'

When I'd opened the door for them, they dragged their heels down the corridor. Had I forgotten something? I stood at the half-open door wondering. I heard another door open and a laugh. Whitey? Did I hear 'whitey'?

I wasn't sure and I went to lie down again. But I couldn't sleep. I thought of last term's final departmental meeting. We'd sat round the glass-topped table, drinking tea and eating lemon meringue pie while outside the students marched gleefully round the building. The dean's secretary had appeared at the door every five minutes with a news update. Her latest: the security guards had locked the building from the outside, as well as the steel gates, and they were going to dig themselves in at the security headquarters. We couldn't get out and the students couldn't get in. So we ate lemon meringue pie. They surely wouldn't petrol bomb the same building after only two years, we speculated.

Later, a thunder shower had sent the students rushing good-humouredly for cover in their hostels.

I'd gone to my office (the rector had forbidden lecturers to go home) and rang my Multiplex agent. 'Is my car covered for stoning?' I'd asked.

'Unrest damage? You're the fourth chap to phone us

from the campus this morning. What's going on there?'

Now I lay listening to the Holiday Inn noises. I heard the splash of Old Spice, lavatories flushing, razor blades scraping over chins, wardrobe doors opening and closing.

I wanted to sleep, but the sweet and sour flavour of lemon meringue pie kept my mind wandering, restless, wakeful.

I am standing in uniform, to the left front of a battalion, against the gaping black background of Africa.

It is cold; a sharp wind tugs at the hair sticking out under my beret. The descending chopper, coming in to land behind us, churns up a breeze. The Leader has arrived in a black suit and Africa's version of a bowler hat.

We are not to look round at the chopper. The Leader climbs out (the slap of palms against R-1s from the present-arms squad tells us that) and appears in our line of vision. Holding his hat on with one hand, he walks to a small steel podium, with a microphone and a table but no chair. From there he addresses us in strong language: the Calling, the Onslaught, the War, the Situation. Then he falls to praying. Army-wise, we close our eyes: onetwothreeonetwothree-onetwothree-Dear Lord! The Leader's praying voice wrestles with the wind, grows louder, whips up our faith against the forces of darkness. His voice booms out even louder. Against regulations, I cautiously open my eyes: the Leader is easing his way back to the waiting chopper; its blades are already turning. The prayer and his voice are a recording. Our squads stand transported, calling out to God with the electronic voice of the Leader while the throttles in the giant chopper are opened up, and it slowly lifts and peels away, leaving me with an indescribable feeling of betrayal, melancholy, rage and loneliness.

The Leader has deserted us and we have to get on with the War.

Which I then commence to do in an inhospitable landscape between sand and sea. My tracker is a black man, as big as the stereotyped Negro common in American thrillers. My firearm cracks out twice and two blacks perish in the swampy reedbed. We draw closer. I bend over the corpses, rolling one over.

'But they aren't combatants!' I cry out, looking to the black tracker for clarification.

He stands a little way off, under a tree.

'No comment,' he says.

Whereupon, without weapons or boots (at the same time the Defence Force appoints a Boot Designer who, with the most advanced laboratory equipment at his disposal, is to design a Boot for the Feet of the Troops; this Boot, buffed to a sublime gloss, enthroned on a pedestal of gold and lit from all sides, is then presented to the press and the nation at a gala function: it is the best Boot in the world) I land up in the long road in a small town, somewhere between the North and South. Exhausted refugees trudge south (in these days the index of suffering in the particular area is the highest in the world – even higher than the Horn of Africa or the Plains of Afghanistan).

'Where is South?' I ask. No one answers, they avoid me. They are weary, I can see that: women with shawls, men on disappointed crutches. The street stretches on endlessly. The gates to the houses hang rusted in disuse, the sidewalks are overgrown. There is no one in the fields. I walk a kilometre or so and sit down listlessly at the side of the road.

The Actor comes by in his snow-white three-piece suit and cream shoes. Just as slick in person as he is on television, he is a gambler with a gold pen sticking out of his top pocket and a red handkerchief arranged conspicuously behind it.

'Come!' he calls in theatrical tones. 'Come!' echoes the

drama school rehearsal area to his call. I am unwilling, but he beckons me to a large building beside the road. It is a hangar or a political meeting place, massive, with only one door. While footsore people stumble southwards, he leads me in through the door. The shining floor is endless. We walk across the immeasurable surface to the middle of the hall where the only item of furniture stands.

'Shall we begin?' the Actor asks me, rubbing his hands together, watching me expectantly. It is a gaming table with a purple leather surface and a dizzying red machine.

I was awoken by the ringing telephone, and shot out from between the sheets. It was already two in the afternoon. My debaters!

It was Edwin; he lectured at another university, even further north. He'd just arrived with three more competitors.

'Have you heard the news?' he asked. 'There's trouble in QwaQwa and the competition has been postponed until tomorrow evening.'

Another day on the plains, and I was already perishing from agoraphobia.

'Hello? Are you still there?' asked Edwin.

'More or less. We had to drive through the night. The student council would only release my chaps in the late afternoon – there was a Biko thing.'

'We'd better have a snort.'

'Absolutely.'

We sat at a small table in the centre of the deserted dining-room. The bar was closed; it was the small hours of the morning and bitterly cold. At the front desk the receptionist sat reading in a pool of yellow light. He'd given us permission to move in here with our cigarettes and a couple of bottles of wine.

'A bunch of ours were deported. Boof, out,' said Edwin leaning towards me confidentially. The backwoods had left its mark on him; he was considerably thinner than he'd been when I'd last seen him. His hair was slightly greasy, although at that time he was something of a campus dandy.

'And down your way?' he asked.

I shook my head. 'The tribal influence is still strong. Although the UDF is making slow but steady inroads.'

He took another swig of wine. 'Boof, can you believe it? Boof, just like that.'

His head dropped into his hands. 'April is the cruellest month.'

'I want to give you something to read,' said Edwin.

'What?' A pot of plastic flowers stood between us. The pink and powder-blue petals were a little dusty.

'Just read it.'

I read.

Today, as Providence decreed, was the day the President had to consider Power. He held it in his hand like the gear lever of a powerful car. It flared up in his heart, a spark that would never dim, when the band played for him and the parade marched for him.

No one would deny that the President had great responsibilities. Oh no, as Leader of the Armed Forces and the Loyal Citizenry and as Defender of the Freedom of the Remotest Village, he was never free from the thing which shone in other people's eyes when they looked to him. He would only be free, he thought this morning, when there were no more followers to look up to him. But it was impossible that this should ever come to pass because, in terms of the National Constitution, he was Leader for life, and he couldn't stay cloistered in the official Residence away from his followers for the remainder of that life.

So today was the day that the President stayed at home, lounging on the purple pillows of the presidential suite and contemplating the white helmets of his bodyguards outside on the lawns.

What went through the President's mind on such a day? As first citizen, chancellor, father and family man, believer and head of the army?

One could only guess.

And hastily add: the President's thoughts were not the thoughts of an ordinary man.

I looked up. 'What do you think?' asked Edwin eagerly.

'What is this?'

He shrugged, slopping a little wine on the tablecloth. 'The start', he said, 'of … well, something. Perhaps a short story?'

I lit a cigarette. 'It's crap.'

He watched me, his expression unchanged.

'Except,' I added, 'that it reminds me of a dream I had today.'

'A dream?' The words were starting to slur.

The tarred road to QwaQwa runs through golden-brown grasslands in the foothills of the Drakensberg. A clear ribbon of water, as cold as quicksilver, meanders through the swaying grass in a stream without banks. It flows beneath the road and curves away in the sunlight and the grass. The wind blows silently over the brown land.

At the turn-off, where we left the Golden Gate road, the skeleton of a new campus was under construction. It looked impressive, rising on the naked winter veld, in the middle of nowhere, a compromise between the barbed-wire capital of QwaQwa, Phuthaditjhaba, and the Free State town of Harrismith.

We approached the capital. It was an extended township, with innumerable houses melting into the fog of smoke. My two students smiled wryly as we drove under a huge Mastertreads advertisement which arched over the road in the form of a huge tyre.

'The Supreme Court,' joked Mr M, the extrovert. Mr P laughed feebly, straightening his tie. They were neatly dressed; on their knees each of them had one of the files that had been delivered to our rooms that morning. Inside they bore the name of an insurance company. There was also a pen engraved with the name of a bank, and a small writing pad with a local bookshop's name and slogan, along with the debating programme and the names of all the universities taking part in this competition for students of 'other tongues': the University of Transkei, the University of Fort Hare, the University of the North …

'That is where', said Mr M, pointing to the rim of the mountain range that lay beyond the sprawling squatter camp, 'the fighters come over the mountains from Lesotho.'

'Really?' I asked. 'From Lesotho too?'

'Yes,' he said. 'At night, while we're all asleep.'

And those mountains still bear the scars of wagon wheels, I thought.

We drove past a few light industrial sites: small barbed-wire allotments with prefab buildings and piles of rubbish in their backyards. I thought about my dream: Did the corpses that I rolled over with the toe of my boot have faces?

Phuthaditjhaba's ministerial mansions were on top of a hill, with a commanding view of resettlement blight and nearby mountains, including the flat-topped mesa, a near replica of Cape Town's Table Mountain, which gives QwaQwa its name and stands as a symbolic barrier to white South Africa. There was a gate and a guard-house at the only gap in the chain-metal fence surrounding the compound. Each residence came with a high Alpine gable and a three-car garage. A swimming pool and a tennis court were under construction. Across a ravine that was filled with shanties there was another compound, visible through the fence, with a fence of its own and houses that were noticeably less opulent. This was the segregated enclave for the white officials who advised the QwaQwa cabinet. I was encouraged to wander through the chief minister's residence; then, preoccupied by two questions, I stood for a time on a rear patio where empty pint-size whiskey and brandy bottles were accumulating in a small pile. One question was what would happen to QwaQwa and, specifically, these absurd mansions if the South African system ever collapsed.

'That's where the puppets live,' said Mr M.

'A culture,' Edwin had sighed. 'A culture of barbed-wire and floodlights and fat leaders.'

'Bugger politics,' I'd said, drowsy and half drunk. It was early morning, just after four.

'Politics. Politics. Everything is political. It's like calling out "oxygen, oxygen" all day.'

Outside, the first buses had arrived with their cargoes of workers from QwaQwa. We went to stand at the dining-room windows to watch the workers climbing out, bundled up in thick jackets and balaclavas. Puffs of steam hovered at their mouths.

'We'd better get some kip,' Edwin had said, and as we went to our rooms he'd asked, 'Have you read *Move Your Shadow*?'

Who will notice me, I'd wanted to ask him, if flames lick my hands and I melt into a defeated flickering puddle?

'Do you know the lecturers' slogan for our university?' I asked my travelling companions.

They shook their heads.

'Burning with the desire to know,' I told them.

'Ha-ha,' said Mr M.

Then we were on a single-track road, in amongst the squatter shanties. I had to change down and brake to avoid an immobile day-dreaming donkey on a steep descent with loose gravel. Playing children whistled and waved at us. Eventually, after a few wrong turnings and cul-de-sacs that ended in the bush or against rusty corrugated-iron or a small knot of dumb spectators, we reached the small supermarket, the red telephone booth and after it the shabby signboard: *University*.

As I swung right I saw the first barbed-wire fence. They examined us thoroughly at security. A couple of overloaded Hi-Aces were waved on but we with our remote registration number had to open the boot and sign our names on a list.

We parked on a patch of gravel, next to other cars.

A man approached us. 'Welcome to QwaQwa,' he said. Where are the ivy leaves? I wondered. As we walked over to the small prefabricated building with yellow light already streaming from its windows, I took the elbows of my debaters.

'Go for it,' I said 'You're both bloody good.' They looked at me; both were tense. Even in the chill that bit into flesh at dusk, sweat beaded on Mr M's upper lip.

'We'll flatten them,' he said. 'We'll defend our honour.'

The small table in the corner was festively decked out. A floral arrangement curled about in some artistic dry branches; there was a pitcher of water with a glass, two silver trophies and several packages – they looked like books, gift-wrapped.

The lectern stood at centre front. A big TV-4 camera was rolled forward and its wiring connected. Lights on tripods were focused on the lectern. An excited crowd had packed the hall to the very corners. Children trotted up and down the aisles, babies cried.

Right in front, in three modest rows, sat the handful of whites. I was introduced to them: the minister from Harrismith, the manager of Sanlam, the professor of Afrikaans, the chairman of the local Rapportryers, a colonel from the permanent force. And their wives, who greeted one and then folded their arms.

Arches blaze ahead of me, fuel drums barricade my path. A car lies comically upside down. A shoe lies beside the car's open, mangled door. Flames still lick over the coachwork, duco curls, curls of duco aping the flames, tracks run helter-skelter, tracks that cling to dancing soles.

Who will rescue me?

When Edwin pitched up with his participants, he and I found seats three rows from the back. From here, cynical and hungover, we could observe the proceedings.

The chairman was a Sotho magistrate. He chattered away in a friendly manner, teased the participants about their nerves, and told a couple of jokes at the expense of the handful of Afrikaners. He was playing for time, waiting for the Chief Minister who – we were assured – had a degree in Afrikaans.

But he couldn't hold out indefinitely. The audience started to fidget. Perhaps important business had kept the Chief Minister at his office. We could begin. The first item on the programme was a reading from the scriptures and a prayer. The professor of Afrikaans officiated. He prayed first in Afrikaans and then in Sotho. Approving amen-amens rose around us. When he was done, he came to the back to sit with us. He had previously been a policeman in Kaokoland and then a school inspector in South West. And now he was professor of Afrikaans here in QwaQwa.

Who will know what has become of me? In sad Holiday Inns with plastic flowers, they sit and grope through the night that surrounds them. In this year of teargas and quirts their understanding is muzzled, like their mouths. And the corpses are faceless. Only the Actor, smiling, rubs his hands together.

The cameraman indicated that his camera wasn't getting power. The proceedings were halted, wires were re-arranged; another plug was sought between the tripod legs against the walls. Suddenly the chairman called out in Sotho. Everyone jumped up. The Chief Minister entered through a side door. He smiled winsomely and said 'thank you' in a voice that, surprisingly, filled the hall. He was trailed by a heavy-footed security man.

Once he'd taken up his position, everyone sat down again. Eventually the power supply was restored and a small choir of black children in Voortrekker costumes was ushered in. They wore white bonnets, they danced, they curtsied and twirled under each other's arms and sang Afrikaans folk-songs:

Come on!
Be strong!
There's a nation to lead,
there's a battle to win,
work to be done!
No reaching for favour or fortune,
no straying to left or to right,
just marching without a complaint –
Come on!

And then, amid the applause, their instructor presented herself. She was a Sunday school teacher from Kestell, a neighbouring town. She led her little black lambs from the stage while the audiences cheered them off with raised fluttering hands. The whites too, raised their hands and fluttered joyfully as though this was a revivalist meeting.

I am given a cigarette and ordered: light it! I take a deep pull of dagga from the slopes of the Drakensberg into my lungs. Sweet, narcotic plant, confessions, it hammers against my pounding temples, confessions of a dagga eater! A dagga eater! A dagga eater!

Then the cigarette is snatched from my lips. A heel crushes it. A child's foot, ridiculously small in a woman's shabby shoe. I am doused with petrol. I hold up the palms of my hands, black with tar, to the bystanders. I am a wheel. As he turns, so shall he turn.

'My students have asked me not use the word *necklace* again in class,' the pregnant lecturer had said, leaning clumsily over her stomach to take another mouthful of lemon meringue pie.

'Interesting,' responded the linguist with the goatee. 'It's become a taboo word in that language group.'

I was imagining the professor mounted on a camel, waving to the long shadows of Hereros, when the hall door opened. A squad of pure white students marched in. This was the student council of the University of the Orange Free State, who had been invited to attend the competition, announced the Sotho magistrate. They were late because they couldn't quite find the way. Nervous and self-conscious, they minced to the row of empty seats behind the Chief Minister. The women too wore university blazers over their neat frocks.

While their blonde heads bobbed about and the men straightened their ties, the professor leaned towards me. 'There is a tendency among Afrikaners', he said confidentially, 'to reach out over racial boundaries.' He pursed his lips approvingly. I nodded and nudged Edwin, but he didn't react. He had dozed off, a defence mechanism that dated back to our student days.

The QwaQwa Quintet was summoned. They stood giggling against the rear wall. The chairman tried persuasion first and then ordered them to come forward. They positioned themselves in a semi-circle before the audience.

'Jan Spierewit, Jan Spierewit!' they sang. There were nine of them. Edwin jerked awake beside me. The handful of whites laughed tentatively.

'Good-morning, dear wife!' carolled the choir. The TV-4 man crouched over his zoom lens. 'Good-morning, dear husband, there is coffee in the pot!'

Edwin rubbed his eyes. 'Jan Spierewit!' Giggling, they broke ranks. Two dashed through the nearest exit, the rest stumbled over legs and feet to get to the rear wall. The applause was deafening. The professor stared woodenly ahead, a rigid smile fixed on his face.

Then it was Mr P's turn. He stalked up to the lectern. At first he was very nervous and stumbled over his words. The theatre, he said, was one of the last vehicles for free speech in an oppressed community. The crowd listened attentively. The Chief Minister folded his arms.

'The theatre', pronounced Mr P, getting into his stride, 'is a vehicle of protest and freedom, and it must remain so.'

The professor checked the programme and then said to me, 'Your student?'

The Chief Minister sniffed audibly.

'We-ll,' murmured Edwin, folding the programme into a jet.

The winners each received a trophy. Two winners were announced: a man and a woman. The book prizes were handed over by the chairman of the Rapportryers. We were now to move to the adjacent hall, the master of ceremonies announced, where there'd be something to eat and drink.

Outside the cold took us by surprise. I started shivering. Among the milling crowd, I looked for Mr P and Mr M to congratulate them on their performances.

I found Mr M. 'I'm sorry you didn't win,' I said. 'You spoke well.' We shook hands. 'Where's Mr P?' I asked.

He shook his head. He didn't know. Then someone took him by the elbow and hauled him away.

The local women's organisation had loaded the tables with tinned asparagus, dainty sandwiches, stuffed eggs, cold meats and tiny meatballs. And a bottle-store had laid on the drinks.

Edwin and I stood with the chairman of the Free State student council. He had the clean-cut square jaw and the direct gaze of a head boy. He held his wine glass correctly.

'And does the ASB still avoid politics?' asked Edwin.

'What do you mean, precisely?' asked the student council chairman in a friendly way.

'Well, in our day, the ASB limited itself to student politics,' said Edwin a little too loudly. 'As though the rest of the country didn't exist.'

'That is still the principle,' said the chairman sanctimoniously. 'We feel we simply don't have the knowledge to express opinions on national politics. We leave that to those with more experience.'

Edwin glared at him. 'And the black youth? And the struggle?' he asked, but the chairman had absented himself to go and have a word with the Chief Minister.

At the drinks table I bumped into Mr M again.

'Where is Mr P?' I asked.

He watched me fill my glass.

'Oh, sir.' The tone of his voice made me look up. 'I am

sorry, sir.' And in a flash, in a flash of recognition, I saw at the toe of my boot, on a limp, lifeless neck, the ravaged face of Mr P.

'Where is he, man?'

'He's crossed the mountains, sir. He's gone over to Lesotho.'

We got into our cars to drive back through the labyrinth of roads through the township to the Mastertreads arch where the tar road began. Fires flickered high up against the mountain slopes, against the foothills, in the gorges. Higher up they were more widely dispersed, fewer; one particular one flickered far, fiercely, high up against the dark mountain. It seemed to be burning in the night sky: a flaming star.

I am alone in the car. Mr M has gone in a Hi-Ace bus with other contestants to a party at the Holiday Inn. Before climbing in, he'd come to me and said once again, 'Oh, sir.'

I sit a moment in the empty parking lot in front of the university buildings. Later, when a security guard comes up with his torch to investigate, I turn on the ignition and pull away. Where the road goes up a slight rise, there is smoke, a goat frozen in the beam of the headlights. Marauding dogs. Coal smoke engulfing me.

The Actor comes towards me. Rubbing his hands together. Dressed in his white suit, with the gold pen in the top pocket. Watching me expectantly.

Who will tell my loved ones that I flared like a burning torch in a small land behind the mountains? Who will say that I went the way of all sacrifices down the ages; I am penance and I am chaos?

The Resurrection of Olive

This morning I received the Schreiner documents from Miss Elsabé Bouwer of the Cradock Public Library. She has gone to a great deal of trouble: photographs of the stone tomb on Buffelskop, an issue of the *Nuwe Afrikaner*, photostat copies of papers. And suddenly the waft of sun-baked rock and bruised spekboom leaves that rises from the documents as I spread them out takes me back, with all the discomfort of unresolved memories, to that sad summer.

My love for that corner of the earth was first conceived when I read a brief newspaper report.. I found it in the small town library while I was nursing a burning graze on my knee (bok-bok at school):

'Olive's body was embalmed and placed in a teak coffin, zinc-lined, and after a simple service laid to rest temporarily at Woltemade No 1. Meanwhile the sarcophagus was being built on top of Buffelskop out of ironstone, by a local stonemason, Joe Mann. When everything was ready, Olive's body was brought up by train and at De Aar, Cronwright was waiting with two small coffins. One of the baby and the other of their beloved dog, Nita.

'On 13 August a little procession of friends climbed up Buffelskop, the coffins being carried by ten staunch natives.

'How good it was that Olive should sleep in nature's open temple with its magical beauty and vastness of space.

'Cronwright Schreiner, who spoke a few moving words, ended by repeating a verse from Tennyson's "In Memoriam":

Thy voice is in the rolling air,

I hear thee where the waters run,
Thou standest in the rising sun ...'

Miss Barber had met me limping through the entrance to the Schreiner room earlier that afternoon.

'Have you heard of Olive Schreiner, boy?' she asked, as she had so many times before, peering at me over the top of her spectacles. 'Do they tell you about her at that school of yours?'

I shook my head. No, I indicated, as I had so many times before, faithful to our ritual.

Oh, the free winds of Buffelskop! Where rock kestrels rolled in the thermals over cliff edges, tumbling into the valley, while you stood high on the roof of the world, between warm ironstone and spekboom plants: nothing around you, only wisps of fleecy cloud and Joe Mann's stone paunch.

Miss Barber and I evolved our ritual because every afternoon I had to come and wait in the town library for Ma to collect me for the ride home to the farm.

We went once more to sit in the quiet, sour Schreiner room, next to the handwritten manuscripts in their glass cases, the Victorian severity of Olive's portraits against the walls. I paged through the yellowed books that Miss Barber pushed in front of me. I didn't listen to her incessant chatter in bastardised English and Afrikaans, only picked out a word here and there that sounded familiar. Especially place names: Gannahoek, Kranzplaas (the farm next door to ours, where Olive lived after her marriage to Cronwright), Leliefontein ... At one stage Miss Barber took hold of my forelock and tugged it a couple of times. 'Wake up, boy,' she said. 'Wake up to your heritage. Your mother is English, isn't she?'

And a little later: 'Olive understood this country. *She* could unite. She could write life back into the country ... not those soldiers out there.'

Outside, the soldiers' boots tramped on the town square between the library and the herb garden, with its drooping palm trees and lily pond full of dead frogs. They were practising for the parade that the town council was organising to welcome the Prime Minister. Later, when Miss Barber went off to make herself a cup of coffee (the town gossips reckoned she laced it with a tot of brandy), I tiptoed over the creaking floorboards and went outside. Leaning against one of the library's veranda posts, I watched the soldiers. They'd fallen out and lounged about in small groups on the hot tarmac. They looked bored and smoked idly as they lay with their heads on their helmets or made eyes at the girls who were hastily ducking in and out of cafés and shops.

Photo: Samuel Cronwright (by kind permission of the National English Literary Museum, Grahamstown)

After a while I went inside again. Miss Barber was stamping books and I noticed that she'd put away the volumes we'd been looking through. The polished surfaces of the tables gleamed in the Schreiner room. An ashtray stood in the middle of the main table for anyone in this deserted town, in this time of war and disorder, who would come and read about the woman who lay buried on the mountain beside the railway line between Port Elizabeth and De Aar.

That night I dreamt that Joe Mann and I were rolling fat ironstone rocks off Buffelskop. He was wearing a shabby little khaki hat, and his stonemason's hands were huge and calloused. We stood near the sarcophagus. The stones bounced exuberantly down the hill, crashing past the red candles of aloes, ploughing a path through the spekboom, chiming like the church bells, down, down, down the hill as far as the railway line at its foot, right down to the tracks and the hurtling, smoking locomotives with their dumb, faceless drivers.

We sat on the farmhouse veranda next evening, waiting for Miss Barber and Mr Crafford. The two of them and Pa had formed a small committee to protest against the participation of school children in the ceremony to welcome the Prime Minister.

'The land is dying,' Pa said to Ma as he screwed the head onto the soda-siphon. He squirted soda into plastic glasses and Ma added a dash of Oros, and we stared into the night, cool-drink fizzy in our cheeks. Ma's hair was pinned back in a bun and she wore a light-blue summer frock. I lay on my back, the veranda still glowing with the heat of the day. With my face near a flame-coloured geranium, I looked at the stars, taking deep breaths of geranium scent and thinking about Isabel, the girl at the pharmacy who leaned over me fragrantly, with tumbled hair, to give me cough mixture in a brown paper bag.

The night lay wide around us. Eventually Ma said, 'It's hard to believe the country has got into such a rotten state.'

A shot rang out in the night, jerking us all upright. The bang echoed against Buffelskop and re-echoed in the bowl of the valley. Pa began to worry about our two visitors. He stood at the low veranda wall, hands on his hips, and stared anxiously towards the gate.

We didn't know whether the shot had been fired on our land or on a neighbour's. Once, Pa would most certainly have taken his torch and gun and gone off to investigate. Now he just stood there and finally said, 'We'd better go inside.' But while we were gathering up the plastic glasses, lights appeared on the road and then there were headlights at the gate. 'It's them,' Pa called out happily.

Mr Crafford, who owned the only bookshop in town, wore a sea-green bow-tie for the occasion. Miss Barber looked daunting in high-collared silk. We greeted each other and Ma brought tea into the sitting-room. Then it was time for me to go to bed, and Ma went with me to my room. I lay on my back for a while, thinking about the cadets' month-long practices for the Prime Minister's visit. Later I crept out through my bedroom window and slipped round the house. I slithered on my stomach between the geraniums on the veranda and peered through a gap between the curtains. The windows were wide open, so I could hear everything.

Pa sat in his leather chair, Mr Crafford and Miss Barber on the sofa opposite him. I was stunned when Miss Barber took out a long golden cigarette-holder, fitted a cigarette into it and looked expectantly at Pa. Flustered, he jumped up and struck a match, but in his haste he allowed it to go out, and he had to strike another. He retreated to the sideboard and poured a glass of sherry for each of them.

'And to crown it,' exclaimed Miss Barber indignantly, in

English, 'here in Schreiner country, of all places!'

Mr Crafford's spectacles misted over and he shook his head.

Pa topped up the glasses. A little sherry splashed on the carpet, and Miss Barber ground it in with her heel, just as one would crush a brown beetle.

'And we think we know our country,' she said, suddenly sad. Tears slid down her cheeks (I stretched to see better because I could hardly believe my eyes). She shook a handkerchief from her pocket, blew her nose, and excused herself. I heard the bathroom door shut and immediately afterwards the *whoosh* of the cistern flushing, but above the sound of running water I could hear her sobs. Her cigarette in its long holder lay forgotten in the ashtray. There was a small red lipstick smudge at one end and, at the other, a smouldering worm of ash that grew longer and longer as I heard Ma going to Miss Barber; Pa and Mr Crafford sat in dead silence, waiting.

That night, after Miss Barber and Mr Crafford had left – promising they'd dial our number and let the phone ring three times once they were home safely – Ma and Pa talked in the bathroom, under the impression that I had been asleep for ages.

Pa: 'I can't allow the child to be part of this circus.'

Ma (always cautious): 'But the whole school is involved. If he stays at home now, you know what will happen. I think we must just let him go ahead. He's still too young to ...'

Pa: 'How many others are there like him who are just going along with it because everyone else is going along with it? That is precisely the problem in this district. In the other districts ...'

Ma: 'Oh, come on, he's only a child. Let him go. He's been in bed so much with his chest ... And he got another black eye at school just the other day. I think it must have been that Reitz child. You know how people work their feelings out through their children. And you and Reitz are still arguing about the patrols in the location ...'

To emphasise her point, she waited in silence for a moment, then added, 'And now your child has to be at the receiving end.'

Pa (gentle, as always, when violence was in question): 'Fine, let him go if he wants to. But nevertheless I am going to tell him that we did not force him into this lunacy disguised as education ... so he can look back in later years and remember that he had a choice ...'

And the next morning Pa cornered me on the lawn.

'So, it's the parade next week?'

My beautiful beret! The months of practising! I was one of the best at marching.

'Yes, Pa. On Wednesday.'

'And what are you going to do in the procession?'

'We're only marching, Pa.'

'I see.' We stood like that for a moment. Pa looked at me, I looked at my feet. Then he put an arm round my head and pressed my face to his trouser leg. He walked away and never referred to the parade again in my hearing. But I knew they wrote a letter to the headmaster, and that he went personally to talk to the commandant of the civil defence headquarters next to the gaol.

They circled Pa in the yard like slavering dogs, their shadows like the hands of a clock, round and round they walked. Round him. Round him. I'd have hidden in the voluptuous embrace of Boe (our cook), by the warmth of the wood stove, if I'd been on the farm. I'd have found refuge where she shifted her pots and arranged the black flat-irons on the hottest part of the stove, if I'd not been marching in the procession from the landing strip to the town hall, betraying my father. I'd have nestled in Boe's arms, sucking my thumb, when I heard their gravelly tread round Pa in his desk chair in the yard, in the sun.

Boe had been forced to fetch the desk chair, I heard afterwards. She'd had to carry it out into the sun earlier, while we were still at school, rounding out our berets and eyeing each other jealously: Who had the shiniest belt and bandoleer? Whose fly bulged the most? Who already had hair on his arms?

While the band practised the National Salute in the school hall, they came through the farmyard gate, bellowed orders at the workers to gather and made Pa sit in the yard. While the headmaster-cum-major handed each of us a flag and a Republican Medal, and we romped gleefully over the school grounds, they locked Ma into the study.

For hours on end they interrogated Pa about his plan of action to subvert the loyalty of the youth. Boe made a mug of coffee which she tried to take to Pa but they chased her back into the kitchen. With their dark glasses and the camouflaged fatigues issued at that time to the troops, they paced round Pa, sometimes glaring at the workers who were waiting motionless under the pepper trees near the milking-shed.

Our procession reached the township at about the time Boe came down the kitchen steps with the mug of coffee. We left the landing strip triumphantly, with the cadet band and the floats displaying the Products of the District. The floats represented the agricultural industry: on the first one a merino ram made of cardboard stood between piles of wool; it was followed by a pyramid of lucerne bales; then a dairy float with a lowing Jersey cow surrounded by bags of buttermilk rusks, polished milk-cans and giant red-skinned cheeses from the cheese factory; a fruit and vegetables float was piled high with produce from the irrigation farms to the south of town.

We expected to be greeted by admiring black faces as we entered the township – the town council had decreed that every employer should give his workers the day off. But the township was a ghost town. Dogs whined on chains. Papers flapped against the fences. Doors and curtains were closed tightly. At one house, on the corner where we had to turn right, a baby started to cry behind the closed door.

In the town hall the Prime Minister addressed us on Preserving Our Heritage and the Onslaught against our Country. A cowboy singer with a white Stetson hat sang and then a magician conjured swanky white fantail pigeons out of a hat.

When we poured out of the town hall after the freedom of the town had been bestowed on the Prime Minister, it was Miss Barber's voice, sad and hoarse, that rose in my mind. The musicians in the band stooped to pick up the instruments they'd left outside the hall. The farmers who had towed the floats with tractors and pick-ups stopped dead in their tracks.

Only the skeletons of floats remained on the square. While we'd sung folk-songs and eaten koeksisters and drunk tea in the hall, the black residents of the township had stripped the floats of anything edible – and of cardboard, wire and planks that they could use for their shanties, because the rainy season with its violent downpours was on the way.

And it was Miss Barber's sad voice that haunted my ears while I stood with my friends in the warm sun on the square and looked at the pillaged floats:

Thy voice is in the rolling air,
I hear thee where the waters run,
Thou standest in the rising sun ...

Every period in one's life has its own particular texture. With the Schreiner documents here in front of me, as I think back to the fearful nights in the barred and barricaded farmhouse while the railway lines shrivelled like burning straws and the wail of the radio alarm washed through the open windows into the night, I recall the textures of that season: Ma's light-blue summer frock, the sultry fragrance of geraniums, the stone smell of Olive's sarcophagus where I went to sit so often. And the foul breath of death, everywhere. But also life that burrowed out from death – the first maize field that Pa sowed after the government ordered the farmers to grow maize to fill the stomachs of our boys on the border, and the first maize sprout to lift its lid of earth, the wet calf on shaky legs behind its bleeding mother …

And stubbornly the memory persists: round and round and round. Out of the past rises an heroic figure, the man who, in his own farmyard, perhaps gibbering, weeping, begged for the safety of his family, his name, his person.

That summer seemed to have no end. We suffered a great loss through the opening of the gates. In a protest action involving the whole district, every gate to every lucerne field was thrown open and cattle were driven into the warm, lethally green lucerne which was in full flower.

When we came back from town we found our Jerseys browsing, hip high in the lucerne. We ran to them: here and there a cow was already lying groaning, others stood bloated and drunk. As he ran, Pa got out his pocket knife and the blade was ready as he took the last few strides. Cursing the citizen force and the shooting practice where he'd had to waste his time, he sank the blade up to the hilt into the distended belly of cow after cow.

Green stomach juices bubbled out as the cattle deflated like great balloons, and lay with rolling eyes, lowing in pain. We managed to pull some through like this, but others died in pools of blood and foaming stomach acid.

As Pa cleaned the blade of his knife against his trouser leg, a patrol drove in through the gate. A motorbike was in the lead followed by a pick-up with Fanie Onkruid at the wheel and Reitz beside him, then a truck, and then a strange machine that looked almost like a harvester cricket. It was the first time I'd seen one: the wheels were so high, it seemed to be walking on legs. Above, higher than a man, were small windows, and on top, even higher, I could make out the bobbing helmets of the soldiers.

My memories of dreams from that period are stronger than my memories of the reality. It was a dreamed time for me and it will always remain so. Not because the domain of dreams is more beautiful or more sympathetic – but perhaps because then the dreams interpreted reality better than I, a mere child, could do.

Night after night I dreamed of the gaol on the banks of the Fish River. Stony and rough; the gaol where the workers were taken if the patrols caught them on main roads with knives or crowbars.

In my dreams we stormed this Bastille with flashing knives and swaying hurricane lanterns. Boe's son Willempie and I led the attack, and I carried the symbol of our struggle, brandishing it high above our heads: the writer Olive on a cross, with a scarlet turban round her grimacing skull.

My troops wore gumboots – heavy was the tread of the labourers' army! – and with our eventual victory, the authoress rose again and so did Windpomp, Boe's husband, glowing, laughing from the red incinerator of the haystack, brushing glowing straw from his garments, stepping through wisps of red-hot hay, walking with hands full of wheat that dripped melting from his hands.

Dancing joyously in the flames, we released the prisoners. Then we hauled the guards off to the hide-store near the station, over the river, which meant we had to drag them through the shallows of the Fish River. Bloody and muddied, their spluttering heads swayed from side to side as we pulled them along by their boots.

We kicked the hide-merchant's doors open and strode through the suffocating stench of meat and salt straight to the hanging-racks where the freshest sheep- and cow-hides hung, still wet and freshly salted. The hides, with their fine lace-work of veins and streaks of yellow fat, were cool and moist to the touch as we rolled each guard in one and then tied him up with rawhide thongs before loading them all into an empty truck beside the platform.

In the still of the night we waited with our flickering lanterns for the first train. When the time came, we switched the points and hijacked the train, taking the guards by steaming loco to Halesowen, the station beyond Buffelskop, where we arranged them in a giant swastika between the sisal plants, leaving them for the sun to bake dry, to melt the fat, shrinking their hide jackets so that their beastly tongues swelled as the contracting hides embraced them.

This was not a dream to boast about, and I would not have dared tell Ma or Pa. Now, years later, I comfort myself that a child in his fantasies doesn't know the salty flavour of real blood or comprehend the ripping of metal through human flesh.

But I blame my dreams – the dreams of those days as well as my dreams as an adult – on what happened that day when Pa and I stood among the Jerseys, and the patrol with Reitz and Fanie Onkruid came rumbling through the farmyard gate.

Reitz and company strode up to us, grabbed Pa by the shoulder and manhandled him up to the kitchen door. I recall a few soldiers: the son of the service-station owner, Kleinpiet Brilletjies van Altydsomer, Erwin Moolman.

Reitz and Fanie Onkruid blew shrilly on their whistles to call the workers together – they'd scattered in all directions. They were lined up against the stable wall. They had to stand with their hands up while Reitz stalked up and down behind them.

'Who opened the gate?' he yelled.

I pressed myself against Pa's leg; there were green blobs of stomach juice on his trouser. 'Cut it out,' said Pa. 'Cut it out, Reitz. This is my farm. I'll speak to my workers myself.'

'Who opened the fucking gate?' yelled Reitz.

Reitz farmed five sluice-gates higher up the river and he knew our workers. Boe's husband, my friend Willempie's father, was not in the group against the stable wall.

'Where is Windpomp?' he bellowed, and one of his soldiers struck Dries in the back with the butt of his rifle.

'He's out in the veld,' Pa offered.

'Windpomp!'

Reitz set off towards the haystacks. Had Dries's eye, deliberately or accidentally, flickered in that direction?

Reitz stopped in front of the biggest stack. He took out the matches he used to light his pipe. The kitchen door, which had been locked by the soldiers, burst splintering open. Boe ran out screaming. It was the first and the last time I ever saw Boe running. I was startled by the thick pads of flesh on her thighs, the strong shins that kicked under her skirt and were finally exposed as she picked up the skirt and rushed at Reitz howling, 'No, my master, no, my master!'

The stack caught alight; flames darted over the top and up the sides.

No one said a word. Boe stood somewhere in the empty space between the kitchen door, which hung skew on its hinges, and the burning haystack. She did not weep.

Reitz circled round the glowing haystack. Millions of

termites crunched under his tread. 'Ants! Ants! Ants!' I screamed, with my hands over my ears, when he took a pitchfork and stuck it into the red furnace and the fork began to glow from the tips thrust in the hot hay and the glow crept up to Reitz's hands and I knew: if hay was properly stacked, as ours was, it could smoulder for six months, charred on the outside, but if you scraped away the crust, it was molten red and if a wind came up the flames leapt up again, making the haystack into a bonfire that the furthest neighbours could see at night. Reitz's hands were molten scarlet on the pitchfork and his body began to melt and he flowed into his glowing boots and sizzled into a strip of crackling, encircled by his pocket knife, his pipe and the buckle from his belt, while I screamed and pressed my hands to my ears so that I wouldn't hear the ants, and I felt Pa's strong arms pick me up and haul me off and I kicked and tried to crush the ants and later, on Boe's lap, in her warm, plump arms, I forgot the revolvers and the men who carried pistols, governments and the men who govern, spatters of blood against the stable wall, and the scrawny labourers, original inhabitants of the land, whose blood it was.

Boe comforted me, the white man's child, while her Willempie, suddenly thin and worn out, squatted in the shade of the pepper trees and watched us. This action of Boe's, while the soldiers clambered up into their long-legged insect and roared through the gate in a swirl of dust, was the most dreadful thing of all.

In the following days thousands of ants died, roasted to death, too stupid to turn round, obeying the instinct that drove them to their nest under the glowing haystack. Willempie and I watched them, and on the third day we decided upon the resurrection of Olive.

We waited until the spirit had come into the bones. Like

my brave ancestors, the Rebels, who would not bow before the British Empire, I led the assault with an ostrich feather in my hat. The bandoleer across my chest was made from a perished girth and old shoe-leather. My heart swelled with purpose: we were going to abduct Death himself, away from the cold domain of rock. I would bring the authoress back to life: Forward, rebels! For freedom and life and the colours of our flag!

Ma had made our flag from a large Piet Retief tobacco bag, with the Dingaan shield and assegaai in the middle and below it the motto of our republic: *Choice Quality Assegaai!*

First we went to the haystack. The wind had dropped. Beneath the heat haze and the black crust the furnace was consuming Windpomp, the wandering shearer, who had come to put down roots on our farm with his wife and son. Then we tackled the long slog over the plains, clambered over the railway fence, hopped over the bright tracks, and started to climb up the steep slope of Buffelskop.

We sat and rested for a little while on the sarcophagus, the rock warm under our buttocks. Then we got to work. Without any difficulty we moved the first two loose rocks aside. I crawled into the coolness within, gathered the bones together and passed them out. In the sunlight, next to the sarcophagus after our sweaty struggle, the bones made a pathetic heap. Badly weathered, they lay on the open sack as if many hands down the years had taken hold of them, fingered them and then put them back.

I carefully packed the bones in the sack while Willempie held it open. Sparks shot out of them, just like flint, when they struck or rubbed against each other. We could smell gunpowder! I wiped my hands on my khaki pants. We hid our horror from one another, for the sublime breezes of Buffelskop were playing in our hair and a flock of storks drifted dreamily below us across the floor of the valley, following the course of the Fish.

The bones tinkled faintly as we carried them down the mountain slope. There's life in them, Joe Mann! sang the wind. Miss Barber was right, whispered the stones and the kriedoring. It was a heavy load and we had to shift it from one shoulder to the other. At the railway line, we had to wait for a train to pass. The loco came from the direction of Port Elizabeth, its headlight ablaze, roaring past with pumping pistons. The conductor waved to us.

Behind the sisal avenue, between the stone cairns of workers' graves, we laid the sack down. From among the sisal aloes, we hauled out the cross we had made from old fencing-droppers and a sawn-down telephone pole. We laid the bones out carefully on the sack. The sun was high and burning down. We argued over the precise position of every bone. Willempie had to go to the farmyard to fetch pliers and wire, while I kept vigil with the bones. The skeleton was not complete: one arm was – crazily – only shoulder and hand with fingerbones.

Uneasiness crept over me. The skull stared fixedly at me.

It seemed ages before Willempie returned. 'Did Pa see you?' I asked anxiously. Pa. Something in him had died with Windpomp's death. He wandered incessantly about the house. Once he collapsed near the telephone and Ma had to revive him and help him to bed. He lay there tossing his head on his pillow.

Willempie shook his head: he had come away without being seen. He set to work. First he wove the shiny copper wire between the loose teeth, drawing the lower jaw up near the ear-sockets, wiring a few loose cranial plates together. The ribcage was more difficult. Why were there so few ribs? 'Because she's a woman,' said Willempie.

Lower down against the cross, the thigh and shin bones. Then the arms, outstretched with every small fingerbone in place. Willempie had hardly finished when we'd fallen in love with her and worshipped her. Using my old pocket knife, I carefully cut open the dress that I'd pinched from the back of Ma's wardrobe. Reverently, we wrapped it round her shoulders, her lovely slim neck, round her pretty hips, her legs, her delicate, tender feet. We folded the dress over her breasts and sewed it up painstakingly with needle and baling twine, finally smoothing the material properly in place, and raised the writer up.

Her silhouette echoed the shapes of the tall sisal flower-stems around us. We gazed at her. We waited. The smell of the smouldering haystack wafted to us on the wind. I thought about the portraits in the Schreiner room; the sour smell of the books that Miss Barber opened before me. I thought about Pa and the Prime Minister and the shots that echoed against Buffelskop at night and Miss Barber saying, '*She* could unite. She could write life back into the country ...' Was it true that the country was dying, without our realising it, and that the Prime Minister and the head-master and everyone at the parade just imagined that they knew the country and their love for the land?

Eventually we got bored and wandered off for a swim in the river, splashing about in the clear water. It was late afternoon but I was afraid to go home; perhaps Pa would be lying as he had been yesterday – as quiet as a dead person in the bedroom. Perhaps he'd stay like that through the night again, right through until tomorrow and perhaps even longer, through tomorrow as well.

As dusk silvered the water over, we sat beside each other masturbating. We both worked vigorously, but Willempie won: his shiny seed spurted in an arc right into the evening waters of the Fish.

I thought again about what Pa had said: 'The government is falling. Only a man who is falling pulls everyone else down with him like this.'

I looked at Willempie, who was pulling his pants up,

satisfied. 'That lady', I told him, 'will bring new life. Wait and see.'

What more can I say now, nearly two decades later? Is the country, or this story, still dying on my hands? Two things remain certain: The writer, motionless between the sisal aloes, where the winds of the Karoo howled stories through her skull that whole summer long. And the haystack, which glowed right through the rainy season and deep into the winter.

No one ever discovered Olive. On one of the last days of that season, Willempie and I sat among the sisal aloes. We gazed up at her reverently. The prickly pears near the sisal avenue had burst unexpectedly into bloom that morning and the bees buzzed around the coloured fluff.

It was quiet on the farm; almost all farming activity had ceased.

'Your wiring is holding out well, Willempie,' I said.

He nodded.

Then we heard footsteps approaching over the dry veld. We froze. Our shrine was about to be violated! I heard the voices of Pa, Ma and Miss Barber. They chatted as they picked their way through the sisal aloes. Had they seen us slipping in there?

We sat still as mice, but when they came into a clearing, they saw us. They stood arms akimbo, looking at us. Miss Barber's face was red from the exertion, as it always was when she came walking on the farm.

I expected her to come up to me and say, 'Have you heard of Olive Schreiner, boy?' But they just smiled at us, waved and, shaking their heads, walked on along one of the many footpaths that they had followed that summer on the neglected farm.

What can I say?

Thy voice is on the rolling air,

I hear thee where the waters run,
Thou standest in the rising sun ...?

Yes, that too.

I push my typewriter back and read Miss Bouwer's letter again (she's the how-manyeth successor to Miss Barber?). On the Cradock Municipality letterhead, she has written, 'Enclosed is the information you requested. I hope and trust that it will be of use to you. I could also recommend *The Re-interment on Buffelskop* by Guy Butler. Copies are obtainable from the National English Literary Museum in Grahamstown.'

I nod and draw the telephone directory nearer. I dial the museum: 27042.

Glossary

ASB an association of Afrikaner students
bok-bok a schoolboy game
bokkems small salted fish
brilletjies little spectacles
Casspir police combat vehicle used in townships
Die Stem current national anthem of the Republic of South Africa
dagga marijuana
dassie rock rabbit
Khaki Boer name for British soldiers during the Anglo–Boer War
kleinbaas young master
knobkerrie cudgel
kwedini children
MK Mkhonto weSizwe, armed wing of the ANC
Nusas National Union of South African Students
Rapportryers an association of prominent Afrikaner business and cultural leaders (men only)
riempies small rawhide thongs
Spierewit 'snow white', a play on the Afrikaans folk-song 'Jan Pierewiet'
SACP South African Communist Party
SADF South African Defence Force
SATV television service of the South African Broadcasting Corporation
SRC Students' Representative Council
SWAPO South West African People's Organisation
tokkelosh evil spirit (usually manifested as a tiny old man)
UDF United Democratic Front, the largest extra-parliamentary oppositional movement during the 1980s
voessek, voetsak [voertsek] bugger off
volk the (Afrikaner) people or nation
zol hand-rolled dagga cigarette

ALLISON & BUSBY FICTION

Philip Callow
The Magnolia
The Painter's Confessions

Catherine Heath
Lady on the Burning Deck
Behaving Badly

Chester Himes
Cast the First Stone
Collected Stories
The End of a Primitive
Pink Toes
Run Man Run

R. C. Hutchinson
Johanna at Daybreak
Recollection of a Journey

Dan Jacobson
The Evidence of Love

Francis King
Act of Darkness
The Widow

Colin MacInnes
Absolute Beginners
City of Spades
Mr Love and Justice
The Colin MacInnes Omnibus

Indira Mahindra
The End Play

Henry Miller
Quiet Days in Clichy

Adrian Mitchell
The Bodyguard

Susanna Mitchell
The Colour of His Hair

Bill Naughton
Alfie

Dolores Pala
In Search of Mihailo

Boris Pasternak
Zhenia's Childhood

Ishmael Reed
Japanese by Spring
Reckless Eyeballing
The Terrible Threes
The Terrible Twos

Françoise Sagan
Engagements of the Heart
Evasion
Incidental Music
The Leash
The Unmade Bed

Budd Schulberg
The Disenchanted
Love, Action, Laughter and Other Sad Tales
On the Waterfront
What Makes Sammy Run?

Debbie Taylor
The Children Who Sleep by the River

B. Traven
Government
Trozas
The Carreta

Etienne van Heerden
Ancestral Voices